Single Against Your Will....12 Things That Keep You Single

By: Beverley W. Haynes

PREFACE

Single Against Your Will....12 Things That Keep You Single is about four single female friends who realize that their attitudes, beliefs, and behaviors about dating are keeping them single. Find out: who could lose the love of their life, whose past could keep them from being loved, whose desperation for love causes pain and whose unforgiveness keeps them single.

The twelve things that keep women single are discussed as the characters experience various dating scenarios. Each of the characters has her own issues to deal with. There is betrayal, regrets, laughter, and tears. Each chapter is followed by a "reflection." It includes: a definition, summary, signs, and solutions. Use this section as a guide when you evaluate your perspective and practices of dating.

What is the inspiration behind *Single Against Your Will...?* After one negative dating experience too many, I realized that something was wrong. I took a break from dating to figure out why. I reflected on my years of dating and the experiences I had, both good and not so good. What I realized was, the bulk of my negative dating experiences stemmed from what I allowed, over looked, or wasn't prepared for. To have different experiences, I knew that I had to have a different *Dating Blue Print*. There is an art to dating and I believe that everyone should create a *Dating Blue Print* in order to have the dating experiences they desire.

Once I discovered the source of my negative dating experiences, I realized that there had to be others who could relate. With that being the case, I felt compelled to create a tool that could help them discover the reason and solution to their dating dilemmas. After months of brainstorming and interviewing men, I used my creativity and life lessons to create a list of twelve things that keep women single.

My hope is that everyone who reads this book will be enlightened, transformed, and entertained.

Table of Contents

Carmen Roster ~ Writer ~ Known in the group as "A Man Hater."
Negative dating experiences cause her to be suspicious of the men she
meets. She declares publicly that she wants nothing to do with a man
romantically. In private, she desires to have companionship. Although
she may sometimes bicker with her friends, she will be the first to defend
and protect them.

Danika Winter ~ Investment Banker ~ Known in the group as "A Jerk
Magnet." Low self-esteem causes her to attract the wrong men. As a
result, she has negative dating experiences that further lower her self-
esteem. Regardless of the experiences, she won't give up on love. She
is the rock of the group. Despite how she feels about herself, she
supports her friends.

Penny Fontaine ~ Fashion Blogger ~ Known in the group as "Ms. Non-
committing 'Penny Fabulous' Fontaine." Men are very attracted to her
and she gets asked out regularly. As a child, she saw many women in
her family being mistreated by their husbands. As a result, she has
chosen not to marry, in order to avoid being forced to live in a bad
marriage. Her heart's desire is to love with no restrictions and to be
loved genuinely. She has the gift of seeing people as they really are.
She does not hesitate to tell her friends when someone is not right or is
up to no good.

Jamie Ellsworth ~ Restaurant Owner ~ Known as "The Man Chaser."
She doesn't have dating standards and will date almost any guy. How
she dates makes her feel borderline desperate. She's saddened by her
self-sabotaging actions. This is something that her friends cannot see.
The one thing that she desires is to be with her one true love. She uses
generosity toward her friends to cover her pain.

5

Boy Can You Pick 'Em

(#1 Not Listening to Your Gut)

Jamie's restaurant, *The Fox Fire* has become a regular meeting place to have lunch with her friends Carmen, Danika, and Penny. Although the lunch crowd was keeping Jamie busy as usual, she grabs a few minutes to join them.

Carmen couldn't wait to have her lunch time laugh. Danika was sure to provide a comedy show to go along with their meals. Her love life was better than any television show. "Danika, tell us about your date last night."

"Uuuuggg. Please don't make me re-live it Carmen."

"Sorry ma'am, you've got to spill it."

"How do you think it went?" Danika rolled her eyes.

"Hmmmm. Based on your reaction, I'd say not too good."

"Not too good? How about AWFUL.COM!?"

They all giggle except Danika. She was way too sad to see any humor in yet another bad date.

Penny's giggle speeds up.

"Penny, why are you giggling so hard? I'm glad you find my dating horrors so amusing."

"Awful.com?" Penny's giggle had turned into a full-fledged laugh. "No surprise there."

"What does that mean?"

"I told you not to go out with him."

"Here we go…Miss Psychic Hotline."

Carmen stops sipping her lemonade and hunches Penny. She knew that this was the opening she needed to get the comedy show started. "Penny, why did you tell her not to go out with him?"

"Something was wrong with him. I didn't know what, but I knew something was wrong."

"So, who was this guy?" Carmen could hardly contain her smile.

"He's just some random guy that she met at the car wash."

"Travis worked at the most reputable luxury car dealership in the city Penny. He wasn't random."

Penny puts her drink down. "Here's what happened. Danika and I were at the car wash across from the dealership on Burton Avenue. This guy in a suit was waiting for his car to finish being detailed. He was talking us to pieces about anything and everything. You know I'm leery of people who talk all of the time. He was such a know- it-all. Shoes - he knew how much companies marked them up. Car washes – He knew what new technology would be introduced this year. Weight loss – He knew which ones were the top money makers."

Carmen was growing impatient. "Now **you're** talking too much. Get to the point."

"Penny, it's my story. Maybe I should tell it."

"Be my guest."

Out of breath, Jamie grabs an empty seat. "Hi you guys. What's happening?"

"I'm being forced to re-live the details of my date from last night."

"Oh yeah? How'd it go?"

7

"It was AWFUL.COM. She should have dug into him like a piñata on day one just like I taught her." Carmen was proud of her ability to *see a man's true intensions.* She calls it *busting the piñata.*

Penny just had to jump in the conversation. "It was horrible as usual. She went out with a guy that I told her she shouldn't go out with."

"Yes you told me, but not everyone has men falling at their feet Miss Penny 'Fabulous' Fontaine. Anyway, (rolling her eyes) when I get to his house…"

"Okay wait." Jamie usually kept quiet during Danika's stories but she had to know why her friend went to this random guy's house. "I'm confused here. Why did you go to his house for the date?"

"He asked me to lunch a few times and I enjoyed his company. We wanted to have an official date, complete with dinner and a movie. I wasn't ready for him to know where I live just yet, which is why I went to his house."

"Ooohhh." The other ladies hummed in unison.

"On the way there, I had this feeling in my gut like I shouldn't go. I don't know what it was but it was there the entire night. When I get there, I called to let him know that I was outside. He comes out, gets in this beat up pick- up truck, backs beside my car and opens the door for me. After the first block I'm thinking he will circle back to the house and get in his car while explaining how he was restoring the truck as a hobby."

Carmen leans in and smiles really big because she knew this was going to get good. "So how many blocks did you guys go before he stopped?"

"All of them. We didn't stop until we were at the restaurant." She looked at her nails with embarrassment.

"Whaaaat? Why didn't you ride in his real car?" Carmen was trying to hold in the giggles but she was having a hard time.

"That *was* his real car."

"Wait, now I'm confused." Penny really was confused. "Why didn't he have a car from the dealership? You said he had a different one every time you saw him for lunch."

"He can only drive them while at work and for work. He says the manager calls him an insurance liability."

"Is it because of his driving record? If so, you know I have a friend who could help him with that." Jamie had a lot of connections and was always willing to help people.

"No it's because of his prison record....grand theft auto."

"Strike one." Penny took a sip of her lemonade and put one finger in the air.

"Now, I'm confused." Carmen leaned back in the chair; this went from funny to confusing. "How can he get a job working for a prestigious luxury car dealership with a record for grand theft auto?"

"His uncle owns the dealership. If you're done interrupting, I'd like to finish. We get to the restaurant and he begins texting in a really intense conversation. To make it worse he begins to flirt with the waitress by complimenting her booty."

"Strike 2." Penny sips her lemonade and holds up two fingers.

"That's lame. I bet breaking open piñatas doesn't seem like such a bad idea now does it?" Carmen raises her glass. "Here's to the art of busting piñatas to prevent lame dates."

They all laugh except Danika. She now realizes her lame date stories are the center of all the dating jokes.

Jamie reaches out to touch Danika's hand when she realizes she's not laughing. "Are you upset for real?"

9

"Yes. This just seems like the same date but with a different guy."

"I would have accidently on purpose, knocked his drink in his lap and walked out Carmen style." Carmen snapped her fingers.

"Carmen you would have shot him down at the car wash." Penny snapped her fingers mimicking Carmen.

"How do you know?"

"Carmen, you are the most man hating - est heterosexual woman on planet earth. That's how I know.

"I just don't have time for the foolish games men play because that's all they do."

"That's not totally true. Just like there are some good women out there, there are some good guys out there too." Penny picked up a piece of bread.

"You should know Penny Fabulous. You break their hearts, turn them into dogs, and they find their way to women like me."

"There's no truth in that. I date a lot because I'm not ready to settle down."

"Okay. Tom and Jerry! Can you stop arguing long enough for me to finish my story? I'm ready to place my order so I can drown my sorrows in comfort food."

"Carmen and I are sorry. Go ahead."

"Don't speak for me." Carmen rolls her eyes at Penny. "Go ahead."

"So after being there for a while, we realize it's about 10:00. He mentions it's getting late and we should get ready to go. I dropped my fork. When I bent down to get it, I saw he was wearing a house arrest ankle bracelet."

"Oh no!" Jamie's heart began to break for Danika when she saw how sad she was.

"Strike 3." Penny sipped her lemonade and held up 3 fingers.

"Hold on. How can he be on house arrest and be out so late but not for work?" Carmen would normally see this as material for a book. However, this was her friend's life.

"I don't know the specifics, but he knows a woman in the parole office who he checks in with when he wants to stay out late and she helps him out. He told her he was at his uncle's birthday party."

"I'm pretty sure that he does something really special for her." Carmen was very sarcastic.

"Carmen, I need for you to have a conversation free of male bashing. The girl had a really bad experience and you're making it worse." Penny was beginning to tire of Carmen's sarcasm.

"I know you didn't Miss I'm done with you and take your heart with you."

"That's a good one Carmen." Jamie laughs and gives her a high-five.

"Yes….and right off the top of my head too." Carmen laughs and gives Jamie another high-five.

"Oh you want to go there?" Penny leans forward.

"Miss Fontaine this is not what you want."

"Well, I *want* to finish my story." Danika puts her hands on her hips.

Carmen and Penny roll their eyes at each other and said… "Go ahead."

Danika sips the last of her drink. "He said that he had been texting his parole officer all night. He wanted to tell me about the bracelet but didn't want to run me off."

11

"We can understand why that made the date so horrible." Jamie shook her head.

"Nope, that's not it. You'll never guess what happened next."

"The police came in and arrested him for breaking curfew." Penny sipped her drink.

"Yes. How did you know?"

"Strike 4." Penny whispered and shook her head. The pain and embarrassment on her friend's face was heart wrenching.

"I was left with the check and no way home."

"Why didn't you call me to give you a ride home?" Carmen was upset at this point. No one messes over her friends.

"Carmen, I wasn't ready to talk about it."

Jamie had her hands on her hips looking at Danika. "Why didn't you call me for a ride home?"

"I knew you'd be crying more than I would be."

"Why didn't you call me for a ride home?"

"Penny….I just didn't want to hear you say 'I told you so'. Besides I didn't want anyone else to know. How did you find out anyway?"

"A friend told me. He was an officer who picked up your date."

"Danika, I'm so sorry that you went through that. I'll have the chef to fix your favorite meal." Jamie knew what would make her smile.

"How did you get back home?" Carmen drank the last of her water and signaled for the waiter so she could get more.

"An officer Jenkins drove me home."

"Thomas is a nice man isn't he?"

"Is he your latest boo Penny? Carmen drank from her fresh glass of water.

Penny smiled and winked. "For now."

Carmen just shook her head.

"I don't know what my problem is you guys. I think I should take a break from dating for a while. At least until I figure out why I'm attracting the wrong kind of men. It seems as if I only date guys who lie, use me, and break my heart."

"Taking a break from dating isn't a bad idea. You can use this time to talk with God about it. You can use my cabin in the mountains for a get-away." Jamie rubs her shoulder. "If you guys want your usual orders, I'll go ahead and put them in."

Danika folded her napkin to avoid making eye contact. Any more sad looks would cause her to break down and cry. "Boy, can I pick'em."

REFLECTION

Not Listening to Your Gut: Ignoring an inner feeling that you should/shouldn't do something.

Danika had a gut feeling that she didn't need to go out on the date, yet she went anyway. If she had paid attention to that feeling, then the entire evening would have been avoided. Her desire to date was overriding her gut feeling and probably obvious signs.

It's possible we've met someone or been out on a date and had a feeling that something just wasn't right. That was our gut, woman's intuition or even God letting us know that there is an issue at hand. The best thing to do is to not go out with that person until we find out what our "gut" is trying to tell us.

Signs that you are not listening to your gut:

- You notice that something just isn't right about a date or situation but you continue to go out.
- You believe that you are dating the same guy but with a different name.
- You notice that something isn't right and someone else confirms it, but you date anyway.

Solutions:

- Stop dating that person until you find out what's wrong.
- Look at the obvious signs of the situation i.e. "the handwriting on the wall".

God can speak in many ways, to let us know when things are not right. It's up to us to listen and trust that He knows what's best. Psalm 9:10 ESV – And those who know your name put their trust in you for you O Lord, have not forsaken those who seek you.

Carry On or Checking It

(#2 Baggage Part 1)

Carmen was in the mood to make her famous "Chicken Ontario." She rarely made it because it seemed like an all-day event in the kitchen, but it was so awesome. Besides it would give her a reason to invite some people over. After she checked the pantry for ingredients, she realized that she needed to go to the grocery store.

Once in the grocery store, she pushed the shopping cart down the aisle with focus. She was trying to decide which of the new ingredients to use and it was really turning into work. She was so distracted that she didn't notice the very handsome man who pushed his cart next to hers. He on the other hand, noticed her and made sure that she knew it.

"Hey....the green jar is the better choice."

Startled by the unexpected voice, she nearly dropped both jars. "Oh.... is it the better choice?"

"Yes ma'am it is. The company owns the strawberry farm where they get the strawberries to make the sauce." His phone buzzes but he ignores it.

She gives a small smile. "I had no idea. Please go on."

"I can tell that you're not convinced."

"Not totally." She turns to face him. She was taught that it's rude not to look someone in the eye when they're speaking to you, especially someone so handsome.

"I see you're the type who needs convincing." His phone buzzes again, but he ignores it.

"I may need convincing." Carmen's small smile turns into a bigger one.

"Well, how about this for convincing? I saw an interview with the company's CEO. He mentioned how they used a top of the line organic growing process."

"Well, that would explain their winning awards every year."

"It does. Are you convinced now?"

"I'm putting it in my cart, so I guess I am." She gives him her best I-see-you-checking-me-out smile. "You look familiar. Where have I seen you before?"

"You may have seen me on Channel 5….I report the sports." His phone buzzes again, but he ignores it.

"That's it. I don't keep up with sports or commentating, but I have seen you reporting from time to time. I like what I see."

"So what do you think?"

"What do I think about the show or you?"

"Whichever of the two you'd like to comment on." They laugh. His phone buzzes again, but he ignores it.

"The show is easy to follow and…..you….you know, I can't decide which brand of fresh black pepper to get." She smiles, reaches for the pepper, and hopes she had this flirting thing right.

"Do you need help with that too?"

"I'm sure you've seen an interview on this company too. So what do you have to say?"

"May I say you are beautiful?" He flashes a big smile.

"Yes, you may." They laugh. "Well, go ahead." She was very serious.

"You…Are…Beautiful." He emphasized each word slowly.

16

"Oh stop. You'll make me blush." His phone buzzes yet again, but he ignores it.

"I don't see how your husband let you out of the house. I'd be afraid that someone would see you in a grocery store, ask you out, and you'd have to turn him down."

"Like right now?"

"Yes, like right now."

"Lucky for you, I'm not married."

"Yes, lucky for me. Hi, my name is Carlyle Monroe." He extends his hand.

"Carmen Roster." She reaches out and shakes his hand. He holds it and flashes a million-dollar smile.

"So Ms. Roster, are you a gourmet chef? I see you have a lot of specialty ingredients."

"No, I'm not a chef. I'm a writer."

"Beautiful and intellectual, I'm impressed. What are you working on now?"

"*Vending Machine Lovin'...How to Choose Mr. Right-Now.*"

"That's interesting. It has a catchy title and clear content description."

"It's been fun to write."

"I'd love to take you out to lunch and discuss it further Ms. Roster. That is, if you're interested."

"Lunch sounds good. However, I don't go out with married men."

"I'm not married."

"Engaged?"

"No."

"Girlfriend?"

"No."

"Complicated situation?"

"No."

"Boyfriend?"

"Heck no! I like women and only women."

"I was just checking because you gotta ask now-a-days."

"Yeah, you do, but I'm only interested in women. I'm interested in finding out more about you."

"I see." Carmen wanted to tell him all he wanted to know. However, according to Penny, you should never tell a man a lot about you when you first meet. Leave something for the other dates.

"Would you like to have lunch at the Red River Club sometimes?"

"That would be fine." She is excited but has to maintain her cool. The Red River Club was an upscale restaurant. It was open to the public but mainly the who's who of the city ate there.

"Let me have your number and I'll give you a call to pick a day for lunch."

Carmen froze. It had been a long time since a man had asked her out or even asked for her phone number. There was something she heard about giving a man your phone number. She couldn't remember what it was. Penny told her she needed a *Dating Blue Print* but she didn't listen. Her stomach felt funny. What if he never called? What if he called a few times and stopped? Would it turn out to be like the other times? He seemed nice, but…She just didn't want to be disappointed again.

"Why don't you give me *your* number Mr. Carlyle?"

"Okay but it would actually be better if I got yours because…."

"So, why can't I call you? Do you have something to hide? I see that your phone has been buzzing nonstop. Do you not want someone to know where you are right now?" She wouldn't give him a chance to answer.

"No. I have stories to cover the next two days. I'm not sure of my schedule."

"Uh-huh. What about your phone ringing like crazy. That's the sure sign of a player."

"Player? No, I get sports updates all the time."

"Updates?"

"Yes. It's my job to keep abreast of the latest in sports. That's all."

"Really?" She tries to seem like she isn't convinced.

"Really." If it's better for you, I'll give you my number. Whenever you want to talk call me. However, I won't be able to answer between 2pm & 3pm most week days because I'm on air at the studio. Please leave a message and I'll call back as soon as possible."

"I don't like phone instructions and limitations. It sounds suspicious and controlling." Carmen begins rotating her body away from him. Her stomach is feeling sick.

"I don't know about all of that. I would just like to take you out." He notices she is turning away from him. "How about this? You can come to the studio and watch a recording any day you like. Then we can go to lunch at The Red River. If you don't have a good time, I won't bother you anymore."

She turns toward him and smiles.

"You won't?"

"I won't."

Why was he being so accommodating? She had no way of getting out of it so it looked like she would have to accept the invitation. This made her a little sad. She wanted to go out, but she didn't know how to allow a man to treat her nicely. There goes that feeling in her stomach again. When you don't know what being treated nice feels like, you'll sabotage.

"Just lunch?"

"Just lunch baby girl."

"Baby girl huh?" Her smile faded. "My ex used to call me baby girl when he was lying."

"Oh yeah? Well, I'll make sure I don't call you that anymore. There's nothing worse than being reminded of unpleasant times."

"Thank you."

"Whatever you need."

That was magic to her ears. She always wanted to have someone who was attentive to her needs. Not to worship or be obsessed, but show that her feelings mattered. She could feel the tension leaving. Could she actually be feeling happiness? She felt vulnerable and didn't like it.

"I can come on Thursday."

"Cool. I'll introduce you to my co-workers. Beware they love to take a lot of selfies so you'll be asked to take some for the company website."

"Yeah. I can see where this is going. I'll pass."

"Did I say something wrong?"

"I know what you're doing. You're trying to have someone to show off to your co-workers."

Carlyle was no longer smiling but had a look of confusion. He didn't know what was happening.

"I'm confused. What did I say to upset you?"

"You said hi. Thanks but no thanks Mr. Monroe."

"Okay, I'm sorry for whatever I said to upset you. Have a good day." He now had an idea of what just happened. He pushes the shopping cart onto the next aisle.

Carmen checks to see if he was still on the aisle. He was gone. "Why do I always do that? It's like I can't help myself. Every time I meet a man, I run him away. It's because of what some jerk did in the past."

There was an older lady who was nearby. She saw the whole ordeal from beginning to ending. There was a look of concern. Carmen realizes she is being watched.

She looks at the lady. "Can I help you or something?"

"No, but maybe I can help you. The pain from your past is holding you hostage and will keep you from your possible future happiness."

"Lady if I wanted advice I would open a fortune cookie."

"Sometimes people will have to see things for themselves. Have a good day." Maintaining her solemn look, the lady pushes her cart down the aisle.

REFLECTION

Baggage: Issues typically from one's past because of negative experiences.

Carmen was allowing baggage from her past to keep her from enjoying lunch with someone who was very interested. She needed help understanding why she was behaving the way that she was. The older lady sharing advice with her was no coincidence. God uses all sorts of ways to talk to us.

Signs That You Have Baggage:

- Constantly bringing up past issues regarding a person or incident.
- Treating a date as if he has already "done you wrong".
- Fighting for your right to be upset over the past.

Solutions:

- Acknowledge the situation(s) that has caused you pain.
- Choose to forgive the person(s) whether they ask you to or not.
- Find the lesson in the situation (there has to be some good to come out of it)
- Try to see if there was something you could have done differently that would cause a different outcome.

Baggage is the result of holding on to negativity. God wants us to let Him handle the things that cause us grief. 1 Peter 5:7 ESV- Casting all your anxieties on him, because he cares for you.

I Don't Want Your Hand-Me-Down Love

(#3 Other People's Negative Experiences)

Penny "Fabulous" Fontaine is working in the office today. She is researching and blogging about the latest fashions. She's on the phone trying to work her magic to score a ticket to the most prestigious fashion show of the month.

"So why can't I have the extra ticket to the B. Rose Fashion Show? Oh really? Well, it seems Katherine that you're not keeping your promise and that makes you a liar. I gave you interns to help you get your shipment out. Now you won't deliver on a favor you promised and offered on your own. Next week when you need help with the Ann Worthy Fall Sample Show, I'll make sure that Kelly Davis is extra busy. Yes. Kelly is on my team. Didn't you know? Oh you think you have an extra ticket? How nice. You'll send it over right away? Awesome....good-bye Katherine." She hangs up the phone and shakes her head. "I don't know why people want to play with me. I have things to do."

Phone rings.

"Yes Catrina."

"You have a delivery."

"Ok, you can bring it back."

"The delivery person insists that you sign for it."

"If it's just a standard delivery, then why can't you sign for it? I'm not expecting anything confidential."

"It's from a florist."

"Flowers? I'm really swamped here and…"

"You would want to sign for these. They come with two teddy bears and one is really fine!"

"All right." Penny mumbles something about being busy. She comes out and sees that one of those teddy bears is Garrison. He is the love of her life. It's been at least 1 year and a half since she's seen him. He didn't see her, so she quickly goes back to the office to get herself together. She wasn't ready for this.

"Oh my gosh. It's Garrison! What is he doing here?" She loses her cool and paces the floor. "I can't believe he's here." She peeked out. He is the only man she ever loved. "Man he's fine. Come on Penny 'Fabulous' Fontaine, get your act together. Mercy….he's the only man that makes me want to cut his grass in high heels, woo!" She takes a deep breath and walks out.

"Well, hello there Garrison."

"Hello, Miss Penny."

They hug briefly. She steps back and looks at him longingly.

"These are for you." He hands her the flowers and teddy bear.

"Thank you Garrison. They're beautiful."

"Fabulous flowers for Penny Fabulous."

She giggles. "Oh stop. So how have you been?"

"I'm well thanks. I see you are too."

"I am yes. So what brings you to visit?"

"You."

"Me? Why?"

"I want you."

24

Catrina the receptionist is being entertained. She leans in because it's about to get good.

"Penny, I won't waste your time. I know it's been a while since we've seen each other but I had to see you. You know how I feel about you. I told you a long time ago and nothing has changed. I've reached a point in my life where I've done everything I've wanted to do. I've traveled the world, experienced things that most people will only dream of, and made even more money than I planned at this age. The only thing that's missing is the love of my life."

"I don't know what to say."

"Say something." Catrina attempts to cover her mouth.

Garrison moves in closer and says in a low, deep voice. "Say you'll think about us."

"I will." Penny could barely get it out. It takes all she has to keep it together when he's near.

"I've been waiting on us for a few years Penny and you've always said that you're not ready but you love me. Well, I'm ready to move on to the next phase of my life. I'm hoping that you'd be in it. If not, I understand. Either way I'm moving forward."

Penny stares silently and looks like a deer in headlights.

"I'm in town for good. Call me if you want to meet for lunch or something. How's that?"

Catrina gives the biggest smile. "That's fine."

"He was talking to me." She looked at Catrina who was pretending to work.

"The number is still the same. I look forward to hearing from you." He gives her a kiss on the hand and leaves the office.

Penny takes the flowers and bear to her office with Catrina following.

"These are beautiful flowers Penny. Do you want me to put them in water?"

Penny is staring out into space. Catrina repeats herself louder.

"These are beautiful. Do you want me to put them in water?"

Penny still doesn't hear her. She is in another world right now.

Catrina takes the bear and pretends that he is talking. She has a conversation with him. "Yes Catrina, please put the flowers in water. You're doing such a great job. I'll make you employee of the year. Complete with one extra week of vacation, a bonus and a raise. How is that?" "Oh I don't know. There are so many other deserving employees and I'm just a spoke in the corporate wheel." "You are the best, Catrina and should be rewarded. How about I go home with you to live since I've been abandoned? Well, ok since no one wants you." She backs away toward the door with the bear. Penny snatches the bear away, laughs and inspects it.

"I just figured it would be ok for me to keep him since you have the man and all."

"I don't have the man....I'm thinking about it Catrina."

"It sure looks like you got him. He poured out his heart, and it seems like it wasn't the first time."

"Yeah, he's expressed himself several times in the past."

"So what's wrong with him? Does he cut his toenails with a knife?"

"No."

"Is he on parole every other year?"

"No."

26

"Does he cut his grass in high heels?"

"No."

"What's the problem?"

"I just don't know how we'll work out because I've seen a lot of unhappy people in marriages and I don't want to be like them."

"So you mean to tell me you're willing to let a fine, smart, fine, attentive, fine, financially stable, fine, goal oriented, fine, all about you, fine, successful, fine, straight man who is kind of cute walk out of your life over what you've seen happen to other people?"

"I don't know anyone who has had a successful marriage. What else can I do?"

"Introduce me to his brother and I'll show you how it's done. That's what you can do."

"He's married."

"A cousin."

"All married."

"What's his granddad like?"

"Catrina!" Penny laughs. "He doesn't know why I won't commit."

"What?! Why not?"

"If we're not going to be together then why tell him my issues."

At this point Catrina is irritated. "You tell him because he wants to know. He was all but begging you to tell him why you don't want him."

"I don't want to drag him down so I..."

"Lead him on, make him feel good but won't commit. I might be over stepping my professional boundaries here but I gotta say this. There are not a lot of single men like him who will open up themselves and be willing to wait for a woman. He is very rare and I know plenty of women who would love an opportunity to have someone to give them half of the genuine attention he gives to you. Apparently, you haven't been in the dating world long; because it's rough out here."

"I date often and I don't see how rough it is."

"True but they don't touch your heart like Garrison does. If so, then you'd be settled. It's time for me to go to lunch but I'll leave you with this. Don't let other people's negative love experiences determine how yours goes. They don't have to live it….you do." She heads out of the door.

Penny looks at the bear and has a conversation with it. "You know she's right. Get it together." "Yes, she is right. I can hardly BEAR it." She laughs at her corny joke.

REFLECTION

Other People's Negative Experiences: The negative experiences or outlook of others determine the happiness of someone else.

Penny had what so many women want. She was loved by the man of her dreams. However, the lessons she learned about love growing up, were keeping her from giving and receiving love.

Signs that other people's negative experiences are influencing your love life:

- You are afraid to take a chance on love because of what you've seen happen to others.
- You think that all men are the same because you've seen a few behave negatively.
- You make excuses for not dating or getting serious because of other's experiences.

Solutions:

- Realize that the experiences of others do not have to be yours.
- Understand that you don't have to permit mistreatment of any kind.
- If your fear is severe, seek professional advice.

It is ok to believe that God will give you a wonderful mate, especially if you believe Him for everything else. Romans 15:13 ESV- May the God of hope fill you with all joy and peace in believing, so that by the power of the Holy Spirit you may abound in hope.

Not Being a Treasure Map

(#4 Not Letting Men Pursue You)

The lunch crowd at The Fox Fire had disappeared. Jamie is helping out in the kitchen since she is short-handed on staff today. Her exhaustion is irrelevant. She has a restaurant to run regardless of her feelings.

She's putting away dishes when the delivery guy approaches with a delivery of fruit and vegetables.

"Excuse me ma'am."

"Well, hi there." Since Jamie is the queen of flirting, she automatically goes into flirt mode.

"Hi, I have a delivery from Morgan's Market."

"Put it right over here."

"Okay."

"I've never seen you before. Where's Brian?"

"He quit." He unloads the delivery, not really paying attention to Jamie.

"Why did he quit."

"I don't know ma'am."

Jamie smiles. She loves it when a man calls her ma'am. "I see you're unloading that fast, like you're in a hurry."

"I'm just trying to get out of your way. Don't want to get you in any trouble because you have a lot of dishes there."

He was really cute. She had to ask him out.

"You're not in my way at all." She moves a little closer. "I kind of know how to get away with things around here."

Her grandmother used to say that women should wait for men to ask them out. Something about men being hunters and wanting to pursue the woman. Well if she waited on a man, she wasn't sure of how often she would go out. She noticed that when she asked a guy out, after a date or two, he stopped calling. Maybe she should just ask out a better caliber of men.

"Well, I have other deliveries to make if you don't mind. I'll finish up and be on my way."

Jamie was so focused on the delivery guy, she didn't notice her cousin Albert had come into the room. She was in full flirt mode.

"No, I don't mind. I was just going to offer you a little something to snack on. I know you're probably in need of nourishment with you using those big strong muscles and all."

"No thanks, I'm on the clock and I need to finish up."

"I know you're on the clock but sometimes we working people have to have nourishment to keep us going."

"I've already had lunch, so I'm fine."

"How about taking time after work to unwind? Surely you do that." By now she is close enough to smell his cologne and boy was it nice. He begins to show signs of being uncomfortable.

"No thanks, I stay busy in the evenings.

"I see...spending time with the wife and kids?"

He's silent and is ignoring her.

"Working out in the gym?"

He realizes that she is not going to stop asking questions. "No wife or kids, just working."

"You're going to work yourself to death. Don't tell me you're a company man?"

The delivery guy finishes up and looks at her. "I like down time like the next person but I think that if we do more than we are paid for then we'll see more opportunities in our careers."

"Good philosophy, but not for what we do."

"Well, this isn't it for me. I take online classes toward my Bachelor's Degree. That's what keeps me busy in the evenings."

"I'm sure you can skip one class so we can go out one weekend. This weekend would be great. We can have brunch and go to a play or something. I also have tickets to a jazz concert."

"Look, I don't know how else to say it. You're attractive and all but I'm not interested. It seems that you're willing to goof off, which shows me that you may not take your job seriously. Besides, you're being very aggressive and sometimes men like a challenge and want to pursue a lady. Also, you're encouraging me to skip class. That shows selfishness not support. If I have time to date it wouldn't be with you. I'm sorry if I've offended you but I don't believe in playing games or giving time to someone who isn't serious about making progress. Would you get the manager to sign for this delivery?"

"I'll sign. She's probably busy." She signs and watches him leave.

Albert walks up and leans against the counter. "Hey."

"Hey."

"I ....uh...I heard what happened."

Jamie's embarrassment did not allow her to face Albert. She handled the dishes again.

"Jamie, you're my favorite cousin so I have to be honest with you. I must say that I don't understand."

"Don't understand what?"

"I don't understand why you acted like an employee and chased after that guy."

"He was cute and I wanted to go out with him. What's so wrong with that?"

"Nothing is wrong with wanting to go out with him. What *is* wrong though, is you pretending to be an employee and pushing yourself on him. It made you look a little desperate."

"What? Desperate?"

"Yes. Believe it or not, some men like to ask women out. They even like to have a little mystery which makes getting to know you fun and exciting."

"Kind of like, how Grandma used to say that men are hunters."

"Yep…that's it."

"I've never looked at it that way. What can I do about it?"

"I can't tell you what you have to do. That's something you've got to figure out for yourself. I will say this though. Start by being your true self and letting the men pursue you. We are hunters by nature and love the thrill of hunting just as much as capturing the prize. So don't take that away from him. Also, it's not cool to pretend. If a guy finds out you're faking, then he probably will lose interest."

"You're a good source for advice. I think I'll keep you around."

"Thanks. You're my favorite cousin. I gotta look out for you."

"You know what else you're good for?"

"Being a male model?"

"No."

"Being a hero in an action flick?"

"No, doing dishes, especially these."

Their laughter fills the kitchen.

Reflection

Not Letting a Man Pursue You: Pursuing the man, taking the initiative when he is supposed to.

Jamie was very interested in the delivery guy, although he didn't seem interested in her. She thought that a little flirting would help him to become interested. The flirting didn't work, instead it backfired. In a case such as this, paying attention to the reaction of the man is an indicator of his interest. His non-response to her flirting was proof he wasn't interested. If she was aware of the indicator then, she would have saved herself some embarrassment and disappointment.

Signs that you are not letting the man pursue you:

- You offer men your phone number without giving them the opportunity to ask you for it.
- You ask them out instead of letting them ask you.
- You initiate relationships instead of letting them tell you that they want to be committed.

SOLUTIONS:

- Build self-confidence.
- Allow men to pursue you.
- Maintain control of your feelings.

You are worth the wait and the pursuit, please believe it. We fall short in dating, when we lose confidence in God's ability to know what's best and to give us His best. We become anxious and fearful then decide to take matters into our own hands. Believe that He will give you what's best. Matthew 6:25 ESV- Therefore I tell you, do not be anxious about your life, what you will eat or what you will drink, nor about your body what you will put on.

Feeling Low….Feeling Blue….I'm Not Worthy

(#5 Not Being Happy With Yourself/Low Self-Esteem)

Danika pulls up to the florist, cuts the car off and leans her head back. She has had a rough day at work. And if she was honest, she's not over the dating fiasco with the guy from the restaurant. It seems as if she's always attracting the wrong men. Her thoughts are interrupted when Penny calls.

"Hello."

"Hey girl."

"Hey."

"Why do you sound like that?"

"Like what?"

"Like you just found out the Easter Bunny wasn't real?"

Danika gasps. "You mean he's not real?????"

"You're silly!" Penny chuckles. "You sound a little down."

"I am. I'm just so unhappy right now."

"Why?"

"I'm unhappy with myself."

"About what?"

"Everything: Dating, Work, Dating, Church Attendance, Dating, Eating Habits, Dating, Volunteering…."

Penny cuts her off…. "Let me guess, dating?"

"How did you know?" They chuckle.

"How long has this been going on?"

"It's been going on for quite a while, really ever since I left Michael alone."

"Are you serious?"

"Yep."

"That's been about 2 years hasn't it?"

"Two years, four months, six weeks, and three days…I'm guessing because I believe in leaving the past in the past."

Penny couldn't help but giggle. Danika knew how to make her laugh even through her own pain.

"This is serious Danika. Have you really been feeling this way since you left Michael alone?"

"Yep."

"What are you feeling?"

"What am I not feeling? I'm feeling guilty, deceitful, and unworthy…every negative feeling imaginable."

"Danika, the affair was over years ago. Why are you still carrying this around?"

"Shhhhhh. Why are you so loud? Who's with you? Are you near a cell tower?"

"I'm at home alone. Why are you having a fit?"

"No one knows except you and I want to keep it that way."

"Okay. So what does the situation have to do with how you're feeling right now?"

"Ever since the situation, I feel like I'm not worthy of having a good man because I had an affair with a married man. Every date I've had since the affair has been really bad. The next one just as bad as the one before. The worse the date, the worse I'd feel, the worse the next date, the worse I'd feel. It seems like a cycle. I wish I knew what was going on."

"You know, a lot of times we know the answer to our own problems."

"What does that mean?"

"You said that you feel like you are not worthy of having a good man because of what happened. That is what you're getting with every guy you date because that's what you expect."

"You made a bad decision and say you've asked God for forgiveness but have you forgiven yourself? Once you do, I'm sure you'll feel better about yourself and will meet men deserving of your time."

"You might be right. It's been like this for so long that I don't know how else to feel."

"Ask God what to do."

Danika realizes that she needs to get into the flower shop before they closed. She gets out and heads in.

"You're right. I don't talk to God like I should, but Grandma said He's one prayer away."

"Yes ma'am."

"I'm at the florist so let me call you back later."

"Okay love."

"See ya." She heads to the counter and is greeted by her favorite florist Annette. Danika has been coming here so long that they've become friends.

"Hi Anette."

"Hi Danika, how are you?"

"I'm great, how are you?"

"Busy as ever but that's a good thing. What can I help you with?"

"I need to get an arrangement for my cousin's friend who just had a baby. I'll look around."

"That's fine. Let me know when you're ready."

Danika browsed through a book of arrangements. She hadn't noticed the guy nearby until he said something to her.

"It smells nice in here. I'm not sure if it's you or the flowers."

"I would hope it's me but it's hard to tell."

"I say it's you. Plus you're pretty like a flower."

This is the part of the conversation where Danika would dig into her dating arsenal. It was full of tips, tricks, cute comebacks, and flirts for all occasions. She's read all the dating books, magazine articles, studied the websites, and had tons of hands-on experience so she was ready. She felt a little different this time. Something wasn't altogether right about this situation.

"A flower, huh?" She smiles.

"Yes ma'am. I'm Blake."

"Danika." She shakes his hand. If only she could shake this knot in her stomach.

"I come here a few times a month. So if you need help, let me know. I could probably get my name in the newsletter for customer of the week."

She giggles and the knot loosens. A funny man was always disarming.

"How many more purchases before you get a uniform?"

"I'm not sure but I've paid enough for the both of us to get a uniform. I'll even be back at the end of the month to pick up boutonnieres for my cousin's wedding."

This is the part where she would say something about marriage to let him know that she's single. However, the last article that she read said you shouldn't mention marriage to a guy you just meet. It will scare them off. Instead she changes the subject.

She looks at the book again. "There are so many choices in here." He moves closer to see what she's looking at. She almost blurted out how good he smelled. "I'm looking for an arrangement for my cousin's best friend. She just had her first baby."

"Here you are sir." Annette brought out an arrangement with "It's a girl" balloons. "Forgot the card. I'll be right back."

"My sister just had a baby too. One day I would like to get married and have kids. Until then, my brand new niece will have to do." Blake lifted the arrangement to inspect it.

"Awesome." Danika tried not to stare but he was a good-looking man with no kids. That was like seeing a purple unicorn driving a convertible while eating a donut…it didn't happen often.

"I was going to ask if your husband or boyfriend sends flowers to your job."

"What makes you think I have either?"

"You're beautiful and impeccably dressed. Why shouldn't you be adored and treated you like a queen?"

"You are observant and smart. Believe it or not I am single."

41

"Well, I guess today is my lucky day. Maybe you would like to join me for coffee sometime. I don't get out a lot and would enjoy another conversation with you. If it's okay, I'd like to have your number."

She gives him her card as Annette comes out and hands Blake his card for the flowers he selected.

Danika feels like she needs to go home and rest. The knot in her stomach was back. "Annette, I've decided on this one." She points to the arrangement in the book.

"Good choice. I just finished making one of those. Marsha, could you bring out the Baby #1 arrangement that I just finished? I'll ring you up over here Danika."

She grabs a greeting card and follows Annette to check-out. "Thanks again Danika." Annette puts the payment in the register. "I'll see you next time."

"You're welcome." Annette heads to the back. When Marsha comes out, she puts the arrangement on the counter and leaves.

Blake moves towards her and she feels a little nauseous. "Miss Danika. It was nice meeting you and I'll give you call. I look forward to talking with you again."

"Same here Blake. Have a good afternoon." She walks outside in a hurry and immediately feels better. As soon as she touches the car door handle, she realized that she forgot the flowers and greeting card.

She walks back in. Annette smiled and pointed at the flowers. "I know...don't laugh." They both laughed. She noticed that she hadn't signed the card. Digging in her purse, she grabbed a pen and wrote.

Marsha comes from the back with two different styled pink bows and walks up to Blake. "Which bow would you like?"

"It doesn't matter."

"I'm sure you're glad that the baby is here."

"I am, yes."

"It seemed as if your wife would never have the baby, but she's finally here."

"Wife?!" Danika forgot for a minute that she was in an establishment. "You said that you were single."

Blake's face no longer had the smile of a proud father but the look of someone who was cold busted. "Let me explain."

"Explain it to the back of my head 'cause I'm outta here chump!"

Danika figured she needed to leave before she really got loud.

Annette looked at Danika's greeting card. "How about I deliver these for you, I'm going that way today." Danika knew something was wrong by the expression on her face. "Why?"

"Since you're a regular we'll deliver it for you, free."

"Annette…why?"

"Your flowers are for Mrs. Tonya Morgan…..so are his." She was looking at Blake. "She's his wife."

"Jesus wept. I think it would be better if you delivered them for me. Thanks Annette." Danika couldn't get to her car fast enough. Once she got inside. She remembered Penny saying she should talk to God about her situation. "Dear God…..it's me Danika."

Reflection

Not being happy with yourself/low self-esteem: Having negative feelings about yourself or not believing that you are worthy of having good things happen to or for you.

Danika was carrying regrets from her past which were a result of her having an affair with a married man. These regrets are the root cause of her having low self-esteem. She doesn't believe that she will have a happy relationship. What she believes, is what she is receiving in her life.

Signs that you're not being happy with yourself/low self-esteem:

- You allow people to treat you negatively.
- You continuously date men who mistreat you.
- You turn down dates because you believe that you don't deserve to enjoy dating.

Solutions:

- Find out what is causing you to have low self-esteem.
- Create a positive way to overcome the cause of your low self-esteem.
- Do not date until you have a positive view of yourself.

You must believe that you are the best thing since donuts. If your self-esteem is trash, then that is what you will attract. I don't believe that God created donuts but I believe that He made us in His likeness. Therefore, we are awesome. Psalm 139: 14 ESV- I praise you, for I am fearfully and wonderfully made.

Baggage Part 2

(Making the New Pay for the Old)

Someone needed to call the newspapers and every major media outlet because this night was definitely news worthy. Carmen Roster is actually on a date! She met Stephen at the bakery while picking up a cake for her cousin's retirement party.

At the bakery, Stephen struck up a conversation, and she laughed the entire time. It was as if he knew she had a bad day and needed to laugh. They exchanged numbers and within 24 hours he called. He thought that when a man is interested in getting to know a woman better, he'll call within 24 hours. Every Monday, he would ask her out for a date on Saturday. It took about three weeks but she agreed.

Normally the work week would drag to a close for Carmen. This time it was different. After accepting Stephen's invitation, Saturday arrived quickly. She slipped on her little black dress and heels with excitement. Her hair and make-up was perfect. As she stood in the mirror, smiling with anticipation, the doorbell rang. Stephen was prompt and looked handsome. He complemented her beauty and presented her with flowers.

She was having a good time on the date. It was going well, maybe a little too well. She thought Stephen was being a perfect gentleman. He was funny, polite, intelligent and very cute. Although she tried not to be giggly like a school girl, she couldn't help it.

This was the best date she had ever been on. She didn't want the night to end. In the back of her mind she feared something would go wrong. All she could do was to wait for something bad to happen. This guy couldn't really be all that perfect. It won't be long before he messed up. She was ready for it because they always did.

Although she was having a good time, something felt weird. He hadn't tried to touch her at all. She was used to guys getting physical at the first

45

possible moment. She's pretty and interesting enough, right? The truth is that he was interested and found her very attractive. No sooner than she got those thoughts out. Things changed.

The waitress approaches their table wearing an employee of the month pin. She turns on her best customer service skills. "Hi, my name is Amber. I'll be serving you today. What can I get you to drink?"

"I'll have the strawberry lemonade." Carmen didn't even look at the drink menu because strawberry lemonade was her favorite.

"Okay, ma'am." "What would you like to drink sir?"

"I'll have the same."

"Are you guys ready to order?"

Carmen was still trying to decide because everything looked so good. "I need more time. You can go ahead Stephen."

"Stephen Connelly?"

"Yes."

"It's me, Amber Fredrick. We went to high school together."

"Oh yeah! It's been like forever. How are you?"

"I've been doing great."

"I saw you modeling an evening dress in *B. Fabulous Magazine*. I don't subscribe, I just saw it while in line at the grocery store, just thumbing through it." He chuckles.

"That's what all the guys say." She chuckles.

"Do you still model?"

"No. It was a one-time deal for a friend who is a budding designer and she won a chance to showcase her dresses."

46

"Awesome! Okay, I'm ready to order."

"Go ahead."

"I think I'll have the grilled Tilapia, Ms. Amber. I've heard it was good, but I also heard the grilled steak medallion was good."

"Are you in the mood for grilled onions or bacon?"

"Bacon...definitely bacon."

"You should get the steak medallion. It is wrapped in slices of smoked Applewood bacon." She points at the menu.

"Okay. I'll have that."

"Good choice sir." It's a popular dish and one of my favorites. We also have a house jalapeno sauce to give it a little kick. I'll bring some on the side for you."

"Thanks."

"Also the rice pilaf-veggie sautéed medley is a popular choice often paired with the steak."

"Ok, I'll take it all. I see why you're employee of the month. Thanks for the suggestions. Please bring an extra plate in case my date wants to sample?"

"Sure, no problem. Ma'am, are you ready to order?"

"Oh, finally noticing little old me?"

"I'm sorry ma'am I didn't realize that you were ready to order."

"Uh-huh. I'll have the salad."

"House or Caesar?

"Whichever."

"What type of dressing?"

"Doesn't matter."

"May I suggest you try the House dressing? Everyone who has the house salad and tried the dressing says it's good."

"Sure, you're super waitress. All of your suggestions are perfect."

"Yes ma'am. I'll put your orders in and will be back in a minute with your drinks." She gathers the menus and heads to the bar.

"Carmen, what's wrong?"

"I should ask you that."

"Nothing is wrong with me. You were kind of rude to the waitress."

"You're right, maybe I should apologize. She wasn't flirting by herself."

"No one was flirting."

"You were calling her Miss Amber and smiling like you won something."

Carmen had forgotten all about how nice Stephen was. She was remembering her ex, Richard though. He was notorious for flirting with waitresses.

"I was just being polite. I called you Miss Carmen when *we* first met didn't I? Remember, you had on the pretty blue dress with gold bag and shoes. You looked like a model and smelled nice."

"You remember all of that?" She smiled a little and was surprised but delighted.

"Yep. As soon as I saw you, I had to find out if you were single."

"Really?" She smiled even more, still surprised and delighted.

48

"Yes. Once I found out you were, I knew then we would come here. I made the reservations that day."

Carmen let her defenses down. She was excited again. Stephen knew how to make her feel special.

"I've put your orders in. I forgot to tell you that we now have the Strawberry Lemonade Kicker if you want to try something a little different."

Carmen was now smiling from ear to ear. "What's in it?" She was ready to apologize to Miss Amber.

"It has fresh lemonade, pureed strawberries with a splash of lemon-lime soda for the kicker. I'll have the bartender add some real lime juice and grenadine too. That's my own special blend. This keeps it from being too sweet."

"Sounds good. Thanks for the extras. I think you'll be waitress of the month again next month Miss Amber."

"I sure hope so, thank you." Amber leaves to put the drink orders in.

"You did it again."

"What?"

"You called her Miss Amber."

"I didn't know I wasn't supposed to."

"I don't like that."

"You never told me you didn't like that. If you had I wouldn't have done it. Now I know & won't do it again. How's that?"

Carmen got a knot in her stomach. The same knot she felt when she went out to dinner with Richard and he would flirt with other women.

49

"I saw how you were looking at her, like I wasn't even here."

"Carmen, I don't think that happened at all. But if I made you feel like that then I apologize."

"IF? IF?....that's exactly what happened. Why did I agree to go with you in the first place. You're no different than those other jerks."

"I'm not like whoever you're talking about. I have even apologized, for something I didn't do."

"Well, all I know is you're awful attentive to the waitress and not to me."

It was happening. The thing that would ruin the date was playing out exactly like she thought it would. Like a train that was going too fast to stop. She knew that Stephen hadn't disrespected her, but she just didn't know how to let a man be nice to her. The "nice" experiences with Richard usually ended with her in tears. It was almost like she was on auto pilot and couldn't help herself. It was time for this to end! The behavior or the date?

"Here you are two strawberry lemonade kickers with lime and grenadine. Is there anything else I get you?"

"No if we need anything we'll let you know *Miss Amber*." Carmen made sure she emphasized her name.

"We have homemade dinner rolls fresh from the oven if you'd like some while you're waiting."

"I said if we need anything we will let you know." Carmen's tone was rude.

"Yes ma'am."

"Amber, I'll take the check now and would you make our orders to go?"

"Yes sir." Amber leaves without asking if they wanted the rolls.

"Carmen, we should end the date. It's apparent you don't want to be here."

He was waiting for her to say something that showed him she wanted to be on the date. All she had to do was say the word. He would act as if nothing had happened.

It took all the strength she had in her not to cry. Water works, right on schedule.

The silence was hard to endure. Someone had to say something.

"Carmen, your behavior has been deliberate. I can also tell that your past is causing you to not trust anyone. I understand. Just remember, every day that you let another person keep you in unhappiness, the longer it will take for you to be happy."

"You're right. It's time for this date to end. I'll take a taxi home." Her tone was very soft and slightly above a whisper. She could not give him eye contact.

"Thank you for spending time with me this evening. Will you text me to let me know that you made it home?"

"Sure."

"I've got the check and please let me pay for your ride home." He left money with the check next to her napkin. "Take care of yourself Miss Carmen."

"Good night."

He leaves without the food. It's hard to eat with no appetite.

Carmen leans back in her seat. It happened just like she thought it would. She remembered something her Grandmother used to say. Make sure that you think of good things, because what you think about the most you'll get.

"Another one bites the dust, huh?" The voice was familiar.

Carmen turns around to see the older lady from the grocery store sitting at a nearby table, looking directly at her.

"Excuse me. Are you talking to me?" Carmen sat straight up. This conversation required her full attention.

"Yes, I'm talking to you. This is the second guy you've deliberately run off."

"I don't know what you're talking about."

"Sure you do. I will leave you alone now since that's what you like but let me share this. Your date was right. Don't let the past keep you single and sad. How do I know? Life, that's how I know." She puts money on her table and leaves.

Carmen leans back again. Maybe this lady was right or just being a busy-body.

"Here are your meals to go." Miss Amber's timing was perfect. She helped Carmen avoid the tears.

Reflection

Baggage Part 2

Carmen has made progress since the episode in the grocery store with Carlyle. She has managed to get rid of a few pieces of baggage and go out on a date. Unfortunately she hasn't gotten rid of enough baggage. She has sabotaged the date because it was going well. Stephen was being a gentleman and treating her like a lady. Baggage has kept her from enjoying nice dates and first class treatment.

When one carries baggage, it can cause paranoia as well as other destructive first-class thoughts. Regardless of how nice Stephen was to Carmen, her baggage created limitations for him.

It is important to get rid of all baggage before trying to date especially if you have negative beliefs about men. If your view of men is not distorted like Carmen's then dating for fun here and there is okay. It can be therapeutic.

Too Picky Penny

(#6 Strict Deal Breakers/Dating Requirements)

Penny sips her chilled apple juice in a champagne glass. She definitely knows how to make a boring Friday night feel special. The great Jazz musician John Coltrane is playing as she cleans her silverware. He is the only man she will hang out with tonight. She almost didn't hear her phone ringing since John Coltrane is on her ring-tone. It was Jamie calling.

"Hello."

"Hi Penny. What's going on?"

"Hi Jamie. What's going on with you?"

"I'm getting ready for my date tonight."

"You sound excited!"

"He's a massage therapist, which means he's good with his hands. So yes, I am excited."

"Girl, you are something else."

"What are you talking about? You know I've got bad feet. Anyway, I was calling to see if you still wanted to go to the antique shops with me tomorrow?"

"Yes ma'am. I'll be rested and ready."

"Is that John Coltrane in the background?"

"Yep."

"Wait. Penny, you only play Coltrane when you're relaxing. Shouldn't you be getting ready for a date?"

"Not tonight. It's Coltrane, chilled apple juice, and silverware cleaning. Lately my Friday nights have been spent with Coltrane and housework."

"I thought you had a date for tonight."

"I did, but things didn't work out."

"What happened?"

"He had too many deal breakers, so I decided not to date him."

"No, No, No!" Not the deal breakers Penny! "Your list of men to date is getting smaller and smaller. If you keep using this strict list of deal breakers, you won't date anymore."

"So I'm not supposed to have standards?"

"Yes you're supposed to have standards, but not the list required to join the CIA. It's like these guys don't stand a chance. What was wrong with him anyway?"

"Everything....He said he lives in a duplex."

"So what's wrong with that Penny?"

"A duplex is an apartment. I only date men who live in a house."

"Oh my gosh Penny really?"

"Also, he drives a four-year old car. That means he's probably broke."

"Are you serious? That's the deal breaker?"

"Yes. There were others but the car and duplex topped the cake."

"Wait, you're telling me that you're not going out with him because he drives a four year old car?"

"Yep."

"How many?"

"How many what?"

"How many cats do you want to keep you company during your Senior Citizen years? Ten or Fifteen?" You will definitely be alone with your *Deal Breaker* list."

"What's wrong with my wanting to date a guy who drives late model cars?"

"Nothing's wrong with it, but should it determine if you go out with a man or not? It's just a date."

"I want a man who has the money to drive a really nice luxury car like me. I prefer a Rolls Royce or Maybach but a late model Mercedes or BMW is acceptable."

"So you're saying that if he doesn't drive a late model luxury car then he doesn't have any money?"

"Yes, because if he had money, then he would have a luxury car."

"Penny, did you think about the fact that maybe he could afford a car like that but has other things to do with his money?"

"Like what?"

"Like saving for a house, retirement, investing to create residual income, starting a business or getting out of debt. You know those things that pay off in the future versus a car that depreciates every year."

"No, I hadn't thought about that."

"One more thing. If he did drive a luxury car, does it mean that he was going to be respectful? Does it mean he would care about your feelings or be a gentleman?"

"No, it doesn't."

"Penny, you are my friend so I'm going to give it to you straight. This deal breaker list of yours might be the reason you're finding yourself home on Friday nights lately. It's just a date not an interview for marriage. How about re-examining the list and base it on things like character, behavior, you know…things of substance."

"I'll think about it. I'm enjoying myself this evening so everything is copasetic."

"Who was this guy and how did you meet him?"

"His name is Randall, and he's an accountant. I met him in my office building a few weeks ago. We'd run into each other at the coffee shop down stairs and he asked me out."

"At least he doesn't work with you. Office romances can be kind of tricky."

"You're right. There was a huge meeting with his company and another company in the building. It lasted two weeks, so I saw him quite a bit."

"Randall…accountant…. What's his last name?"

"Bradley."

"Randall Bradley. Does he work for Timmons & Johnson Accounting Firm?"

"Yeah…how did you know?"

"Go do some research on him."

"I don't have time to do all of that. What is it?"

"Uummm, are you sitting down?"

"What is it?"

"Do you remember Lindsey who does my hair; always bragging about her brother?"

"Yeah."

"He's her brother. Today she showed me the article about a corporate buyout with his accounting firm. Apparently the meeting was spearheaded by Randall and was a total success. The company made more money than expected. As a result Randall was made partner. So now the firm is called Timmons, Johnson & Bradley. Not only did he make partner, she says he owns all the duplexes on his block, and the chain of Bradley Shoes."

The silence from Penny's line made Jamie glad that she told her to sit down.

"Penny, are you still there?"

"Yeah, I, uh....."

"I understand. I'll to talk with you later. My date is at the door. Tell Coltrane that I said hi."

Reflections

Deal Breakers: A list of strict dating characteristics that one's date must possess.

Penny was used to dating regularly. It was also common for her to have strict dating characteristics that each date must possess. It took a lonely Friday night and the view point of someone else to show her that deal breakers may cause her to be single.

Signs that your deal breaker list may be keeping you single:

- If you've had the same deal breaker list for more than 2 years and you rarely date.
- If you never go out because the guys you meet have majority of the lists' characteristics.
- If your list consists mainly of superficial or materialistic things.

Solutions:

- Create a new list based loosely on what you have to offer, what you want and the non-negotiable.
- Do not use other people's expectations.
- Be realistic and remember that no one is perfect.

We know what we want in a mate but do we know why? Are our desires superficial? Are they our own desires? Are they realistic? Why not be more open minded about those who we turn our nose up at because of their finances, looks, back ground or career choice. Matthew 7:1 ESV Judge not, that you not be judged.

OMG He Is....

(#7 Telling Your Friends Everything)

"Are you ladies ready to order?" The waitress had her pen ready to write.

"We need a few minutes to decide please." Danika wasn't really hungry because she had attended a breakfast meeting for work. She was glad to be having lunch with her friend Megan. They met at the beauty salon five years ago and have been buddies ever since.

"Megan, I can't believe you've never seen that movie. It was at the theaters for like three months. I saw it three times."

"Well Danika, I don't get to go out on dates like you."

"If you would get out more you could. Work, church, home, work church, home. Those are the only places you go."

"I can't help it. I don't know how to meet men."

"You don't have to know how to meet them, just be your fabulous self and they will make it their business to meet you."

"Is that how you do it?"

"Yes. Now let me warn you. There may be a lot of guys who aren't what you're looking for, but it doesn't hurt to go out anyway. You can become the best of friends and be introduced through someone they know."

"Wow, sounds like you can teach a class on dating."

"Not me. Penny could though. She shares dating nuggets here and there."

"It sounds like she dates a lot."

"Yeah she goes out a lot. Then shares the do's and don'ts that she learns along the way. It could be beneficial if I actually did what she said. She doesn't go into details about the dates though."

"Why doesn't she go into details? Don't you tell her about your dates?"

"I never asked her why she doesn't go into details."

"What about your other friends, do they share with you like you share?"

"Depends upon what it is."

"I'd be careful if I were you Danika."

"Why?"

"It's not good to tell your friends everything about your dates."

"You always say that."

"It's the truth."

"Why?"

"I've had experiences where I've shared my business and let's just say, I heard it in the street."

"That's awful Megan. My girls are real friends and I don't believe that they would tell my business."

"Okay as long as you know it. Hey what ever happened on your date with that guy from the dealership, what's his name, Travis?"

"Oh my gosh! Let's just say I won't be seeing him again. The date turned out to be a fiasco."

"Really? I remember you telling me you were seeing him for lunch almost every day."

"Yeah....almost every day. We talked on the phone everyday too. He'd text just to say hi and play movie trivia. You know I love movie trivia. He'd send flowers just because."

"He sounds like a nice guy."

"Yeah he is, was, whatever."

"So, how long did he stay in jail?"

"I guess not long because on Monday I saw him driving past the restaurant where I was having lunch."

"Getting arrested, what a way to end a date."

"I know, right? He was...wait....I didn't tell you he was arrested."

"Yes you did."

"When?"

"The other day."

"No ma'am, I did not."

"You must have told me. How else would I know that Bucky went to jail?"

"How did you know that he went by Bucky? That's a family name. Now I know I didn't tell you that."

Megan squirmed a little. She was telling on herself and there seemed no way to undo what happened.

"I'm waiting Megan." Danika was running out of patience. Next, she would use a Carmen scare tactic. Carmen was good at getting the truth out of people.

"I know Bucky....uh Travis."

"Why didn't you tell me you knew him?"

"I just didn't."

"How do you know him?"

Megan stared at her glass. She didn't want to look at Danika because she was afraid of her reaction.

"We dated."

"Is there more?"

"There is."

"Wait, when I told you about him, why didn't you tell me you used to date him?"

Meagan looked around the room. This was starting to get serious.

"Megan, we've always been upfront with each other. So I need for you to be upfront now."

"Need? Why do you need anything? You have all the men, so why do you need anything?"

"What are you talking about?"

"You want to know the truth, well here it is sister. I dated Travis while you were dating him. You're always talking about your dates with these guys. You never tried to introduce me to any of their friends so we could double date. I stayed home alone."

"You never said you wanted to go out on a double date. When I mentioned I had a date, you always said, it must be nice."

"Well if you were really my friend you should have known I wanted to go out too."

"I don't believe this. You dated the man I was dating because you were jealous?"

"If that's how you want to see it."

"Why?"

"You kept talking about how fun and thoughtful he was. How he made you feel happy and special. I wanted that too. Since you were too selfish to introduce me to someone, I introduced myself to Travis."

"You asked me about all my dates. I never volunteered."

"You volunteered with your 3 funky friends though didn't you. They always laugh at you."

"We laugh at each other and we don't date one another's men."

"Maybe if you hadn't blown me off then I wouldn't have to date your man."

"What?!"

"If you would have cared about whether I had a special someone, then I wouldn't have taken Travis from you."

"Oh really?"

"Yes….really. I really liked him. You made it so easy. It seemed like we were already dating. I knew all the things that made him unique and desirable. How could I not want him?"

"Easy. Just remember that he was the guy your friend was dating."

"I know you were wondering how I knew he'd been arrested. I called his parole officer and told her he was out on a date and not at his uncle's party. She was glad to help her cousin punish her cheating boyfriend."

"You are the grimiest, most low down, rotten, no good, ugly, buck tooth...you know what, I think I'll leave."

"No, I'll leave. Travis is meeting me for drinks anyway. I told you not to tell anyone everything about your dates."

"Hope you got bail money."

Meagan stood and walked away with an air of victory.

Danika was glad that Meagan left. She wasn't sure if her legs would hold her up, let alone walk to her car.

The waitress reappeared. "Is there anything that I can get you ma'am?"

"Yes, you can give me a hand and take this knife out of my back."

Reflection

Telling Your Friends Everything: Specifically, telling your friends everything about the man that you're interested in.

Danika had told Megan all about Travis. There is nothing wrong with telling your friends about someone you're interested in. The problem is telling all of the things that make him special. Romanticizing his characteristics especially to someone who is single can be an issue. Although Danika was the victim, she was also the culprit. How is that possible you may be wondering? She confided in another woman about the man whom she was interested in. It is common place for women to share information about the man they're dating. However, it didn't cross Danika's mind that she would be betrayed. If so, then she would have been less confiding.

Signs that you are telling your friends too much:

- Every conversation you have with your friends includes information about him.
- When your friends know just as much about him as you do, because you told them.
- If your friends constantly remind you of his issues.

Solutions:

- Never tell everything about "him" to your friends.
- Never tell anything you don't want the world to know.
- Consider his feelings.

Stop telling everything!!!!!!!!! Ain't nothing deep about this reflection. The more you tell, the more that can come back and haunt you. Proverbs 21:23 ESV - Whoever keeps his mouth and his tongue keeps himself out of trouble.

Show Me How Much You Miss Me

(#8 Giving Up the Goods)

Penny is at Jaime's house bonding. It had been a while since they've had girlfriend time. Although they loved hanging as a group, it was still good to have their time alone.

"So Penny, are you saying I shouldn't go out with him ever again?"

"I'm saying that maybe you should really think about it before you agree to go again. Truth be told Jamie, I don't believe you should. Plus you definitely shouldn't ask him about going out. If a man is interested in a date, he'll ask you."

"Why shouldn't I ask him about going out? I don't want to spend another Saturday night alone. Besides, I miss him. It's been almost three months since I've seen him."

"Well, I can't put my finger on it but something isn't right."

"Uh-oh, here's Penny the Protector."

"I *am* protective of my friends but hey, you are a grown woman. My opinion is just that, an opinion. If you want to go out with him then you do it."

"Don't get me wrong girl, I appreciate your concern but he's a nice guy."

"I understand. My concern is with the fact that every time you've gone out with him, he's tried to get physical."

"You don't have to say it like that!"

"Like what?"

"Like he tried to abuse me or something......*get physical.*" She mocked Penny.

"Didn't you say that at the end of every date he tried to get physical? Those were your words."

"It's natural for a man to want to have sex with a woman. If he didn't express his desire for her how would she know that he was interested?"

"How about tell her, show up on time, pay attention to only her....Do I need to go on?"

"Nope. I got it mama hen."

"Mama hen huh? I can take a hint."

"I wasn't hinting at anything Penny. It's just that you are acting really serious and strict right now."

"It's only because being celibate is important to you and this guy....."

"This guy what? By the way, his name is Sullivan."

"This guy Sullivan..." Penny said with an attitude, "is not someone you should date since he's already shown you he's after the goods."

"Well, as long as I keep the goods locked away then it's all good." Jamie laughs because she thought she made a play on words.

Penny laughs too. It wasn't very funny but the conversation was getting kind of serious.

"Jamie, you know I'm only looking out for you. I've been where you are and....well, never mind. You say you know what you're doing."

"No need to worry. I'm a big girl. Besides, I think he's lost interest."

"Oh really? Why is that?"

"On our last date, he said he was really into me. He wanted to spend the night and cuddle. I said it wasn't a good idea. I was celibate and it would be too much temptation. He got an attitude and accused me of playing games. We haven't gone out since. I've received a text here or there but that's about it."

"Wow. You didn't tell me all that."

"It's embarrassing. How do you explain it to your friends? The one guy who goes out with you, doesn't want to keep his hands to himself? Plus, he can't get with the fact that you're celibate."

"That's bad Jamie. What's worse is that you got along great."

"Well, I guess that's the way it is sometimes."

"I guess it is. Well, I gotta go."

"A date no doubt. Ms. Fontaine always has a date."

"No date….I'm going to the nail salon but I am expecting a call from Garrison."

"Not *The* Garrison!"

"Yep, the one and only, Mr. Garrison."

"Well, hurry up and get out of here. Don't keep him waiting. Tell my friend I say hi."

"I sure will. Call if you need anything."

Penny leaves and Jamie sits at the kitchen counter nibbling on the strawberries. She and Penny always have an array of fruit when it's just the two of them bonding. There was actually enough left over to make some kind of dessert but she really didn't feel like cooking. Ten minutes later, the phone rang. As she got off the stool to get it, she caught a reflection of herself in a mirror. She starred and mumbled,

"When am I going to be with the love of my life?" Picking up the phone, she realized that it was Sullivan.

"I'm not going to answer him." She stares at the caller ID picture.

Finally the phone stopped ringing. She puts it down. Less than one minute later, he calls again.

"Nope." She walks over to the counter and munches on the strawberries. For the next ten minutes she consumes strawberries and ignores Sullivan repeated calls.

"Ugg! I can't take this. I'm cutting it off." She was getting annoyed with his calling. It didn't look like he was going to go away so she answers.

"Hello." She answered with no enthusiasm, no hint of excitement.

"Hi."

Dead silence. This was the longest telephone silence in history.

"How are you Jamie?"

"Who is this?"

"It's Sullivan. Have you forgotten about me already?"

"You got a last name Sullivan?"

"I guess you have."

"What can I do for you?" Jamie thought for a second and wondered how would Carmen handle this? She needed to know what to say because the last conversation didn't go well. If only she could be cold and heartless at the flip of a switch like Carmen.

"You can accept my apology and forgive me for being an insensitive jerk."

71

"Uh-huh."

"Well, I won't bother you anymore. I just wanted to apologize."

"Ok."

"Take care of yourself Jamie."

"All right."

"By the way I left a gift on your door step."

"Okay. Bye"

Jamie was a bit proud of herself for not holding conversation. At the same time, she felt bad. She learned in church that when someone asks for forgiveness you're supposed to forgive. She asks God for forgiveness regularly and believes He does every time.

"I'll call him back later and accept his apology with a sincere heart. Right now I'm upset. Not too upset to let this gift sit outside though."

She heads for the front door and upon opening it; she sees the huge gift basket he's left. It was filled with all of her favorites. There were body care treats, expensive candies, candles, DVD's of her favorite classic TV shows and a bunch of her other favorites. The basket was beautifully arranged and wrapped. It was almost a shame to open it…..almost.

She needed to call Sullivan. At the very least thank him for the gift and accept his apology. After that there would be no need to communicate, right?

She strolls into the kitchen for the phone. All the while she is fighting the urge to be mean to him the way that she'd seen Carmen do.

"Okay Jamie…..deep breath…..go." Her finger presses his name in the call log and the phone makes the connection.

She hears him pick up and she automatically folds her arms. His voice on the other end sounded very professional. "Will this be pick up or delivery?"

Jamie laughs. He caught her off guard. She really missed the way he made her laugh.

"You are so silly Sullivan."

"I just wanted to make you laugh lady."

"Well, you did."

"I'm glad."

There was that silence again.

"So uh, I decided to call and let you know I appreciated the gift basket and accept your apology."

"You're welcome for the gift and thank you for accepting the apology. I shouldn't have given you a reason to have to accept an apology. I've wanted to call just to hear your voice. I've missed you, but I thought you wouldn't talk to me. I was right."

"Well, I finally answered, so there you go. Life is worth living again." She lets out a chuckle.

"I've missed your laugh Jamie." He whispered it so sweetly that she could feel his breath in her ear. She dropped her defenses and sat on the stool at the kitchen counter. What would he say next? Since he was trying to get back into her good graces, it had best to be something captivating.

"Well, I won't keep you. Thanks again for accepting my apology and enjoy the gifts."

"Okay." She was in shock a little and slowly stood up. Penny taught her to stand and hold conversation with a man when you don't want to sound emotional. He seemed like he would not bombard his way back into her life. It seemed about her happiness right now. That was different, even endearing.

"I don't want to take up your time."

Immediately she knew she missed him as much as he missed her. She couldn't tell him. Penny always warned them about showing a man how much you miss him when he's in the dog house. Something about losing leverage.

"Sure, thanks for everything."

"Okay."

"Okay."

"All right."

"All right."

Neither wanted to hang up. Jamie had to think of something quick to keep the conversation going. She knew what Penny said but *shoot*, Penny also had a man who adored her for years. Jamie just wanted one to like her for a few more minutes.

"Delivery."

"What?"

"You said pick up or delivery. Delivery would be the final touch to my gift basket."

"Okay…whatever you want I'll get it." The words seemed to slide off his lips and wrap around her ear. He put a little silky base in his voice.

"Surprise me." She was so nonchalant. At this point, playing it cool was crucial.

"Give me about thirty minutes and I'll be there to deliver your meal."

"Okay," she responded slyly.

Oh snap! Jamie was nowhere near being presentable. She was dressed but that was for Penny, not a man, with her sweats on and barely any make up. The house could stand tidying and her breath smelled like cheese. Thirty minutes wasn't long enough, but it had to be!

She hit the bathroom to freshen up, change clothes, and look extra cute. Only fifteen minutes gone, but she was now presentable. Just enough time to tidy up.

The doorbell rang. Dang! Thirty minutes already? Her heart was beating so fast. When she gets to the door, she feels the butterflies but opens it anyway.

"Excuse me. I have a delivery for the most beautiful woman in the world."

"Well, you are definitely at the right place." They chuckle and she opens the door wider so he could come in. "Right this way." She leads him to the kitchen.

"You have a nice house."

"Thanks."

"All right, where do you want me to put the food?"

"Over here on the counter is fine."

"On the menu tonight is baked ziti, pepperoni calzones with marina dipping sauce, and garlic cheese bread. There's some cake for dessert."

He holds the bag open as she pulls the containers out. "Wow, all of my favorites."

"I remembered that you enjoy eating at the Italian Villa."

"I do. Thank you so much. I'll get the plates."

"That's okay. I have to be going. I wanted to bring you dinner to go with your basket."

"Oh. Well, here let me get you a tip."

She digs into her purse. Out of the corner of her eye, she sees him leaning slowly towards her.

Her heart begins to race. He had that effect on her. She closed her eyes, preparing for a kiss on her cheek.

"Are you okay?"

"What?" She opened her yes. He was eating the strawberry he leaned to get.

"Are you okay? You have your hands in the purse with your eyes closed."

"Yeah uh, I'm fine. I was trying to remember what I did with that cash I had. I gotta give you a tip."

"I don't need a tip. The smile on your face is more than enough."

"Really?" Her smile showed that she believed him.

"Yes. I would like to give you a real apology."

"Okay."

"First, I haven't held a real conversation with you in about three months. A text here and there doesn't count. Second, I wasn't always a gentleman when we went out. I asked you repeatedly to spend some time alone with me. It was something you didn't want to do. I didn't take into consideration the temptation and your being celibate. I could give you this long drawn out explanation but that's lame and unnecessary. The truth is you do something to me. You turn me on and not just physically."

"No? What is it then?" Jamie tried her best not to melt. Their heart to heart talks turned her on. The cologne, his 6ft plus frame and bedroom eyes were ok. But his intellect, compassion and gentleness is what did it for her.

"It's your strength, determination, and mindset."

Mercy! Her knees were getting weak but she had to stand upright and pretend like she was unfazed. "Go on."

"Not a lot of women practice celibacy. However, some of those do give up their celibacy when they get pressured. You never did. It took strength to stand on your morals and cut me off when I didn't respect you. You are rare."

"Well I…." That was all she managed to say because Penny was calling. If she ignored her, then Penny would most likely keep calling or come over. "I've got to answer this."

"Go ahead. I've got to be going anyway. Good seeing you again." He turns towards the door. In an act of reflex, she grabbed his arm. He's been in the gym, she could tell. Maybe he *should* leave.

"I'll just be a minute." She grabbed the phone, stepped into the hallway and answered before the call was fully connected. "Hello, Hello…."

"Uh. Is everything okay? You sound kind of weird."

"Yeah, I'm okay. What's going on?" She peeked into the kitchen. Sullivan helped himself to more strawberries. She had to get Penny off the phone but dared not tell her he was there. Penny and her Magic 8 Ball would say get rid of him *and* the food.

"I think I left my charger at your house and I wanted to come back to get it."

77

"It's not here. I've just finished cleaning and it's not here." She hadn't cleaned anything but Penny could not come back.

"Okay maybe I left it at the nail salon. Garrison's calling. I'll talk with you later."

"All right." She took a deep breath and got her nerves together. Bravery was needed to watch him walk out the door.

"Sorry about that."

"That's ok. I was enjoying the strawberries." He moves toward the door. His cologne would be in the air long after he left. "I appreciate you accepting my gifts and apology."

"You are welcome." She missed him so much. Why did he have to leave?

"I guess, I'll see you around Ms. Jamie."

"Bye Sullivan." He opened the door. "Can I fix you some food to take with you? I can't eat it all."

"That's fine." He closes the door and they head back to kitchen. She washes her hands and gets storage bowls. As she's opening the baked ziti, she takes a fork and feeds him a taste.

"Ummm. This is so good." He takes the fork and feeds her. Back and forth is how it goes until they've made big dents in the ziti.

"Do you want to stay and have a plate?"

"Sure if it's not too much trouble."

"No trouble at all. I can put in one of the DVDs from my gift basket."

She fixes the plates and puts them on the counter. "I'm not sure of how to work the DVD player, I'm ashamed to say."

"No worries. I'm a DVD player expert, regardless of the brand." After fiddling around with it, he figured out how it worked. "Come and let me show you how it works."

When she got to him, there was a haze of something indescribable. It felt as if she was moving in slow motion. He pointed and explained things but she didn't hear. Their eyes locked and her breathing got shallow. He looked away quickly and explained things a little more.

He gave her a quick kiss. "I'm not sorry I did that. If you want me to go I will but I've missed you something awful."

"It might be best if you go. I'll fix your food." She headed to the counter.

He made a few adjustments to the DVD player while she put the food in bowls.

"It was good seeing you again and thank you for accepting my apology."

"You're welcome."

He grabs the bowls and leans in for another quick good-bye kiss. She didn't resist. He kissed her again but longer. He put down the bowls and wrapped her in his embrace. The next kiss was passionate, sincere, and over powering. Time stood still.

"Sullivan, show me how me how much you missed me."

He picked her up and found his way to her bedroom. She experienced pleasure that he'd been waiting months to share with her.

. . . .

Jamie woke up with a smile she knew would remain for as long as these new memories would. Rolling over, she faced Sullivan. His smile was wider than hers.

"Hi."

"Hi." Jamie giggles and gives him a kiss. "I thought we could catch a movie tonight. I'm not sure of what's playing but we can check it out on my phone."

Sullivan rolls out of bed and dresses.

"When you get the phone, would you grab me some water?"

"I, uh, got something I need to take care of in an hour so I'll just go."

The air in the room became thin. Jamie's breathing became more difficult to experience. She knew what was happening but to say it would make it official.

"You're leaving?"

"Yeah." He couldn't get dressed fast enough.

"Okay….I understand." She didn't. He said he missed her something awful, but his sudden departure said something entirely different.

He grabs his keys. "I'll call you later." In no time flat, he was out of the room and down the hallway.

This is the "something isn't right" that Penny warned her about.

One tear fell from her right eye. "But….he….I just….help God…I can't breathe." The reality of the situation engulfed her like an old friend she hoped to never see again. "No! No! No!....how did I….what….why can't…." She jumps up, throws on her clothes, and races for the front door. What would happen when she got there she didn't know. There was no need to open it. She knew that he left.

Her phone rang. It was Penny. Jaime gathered herself and answered, hoping she could hide the pain. "Hey Penny, what's up?"

"I don't know. I just felt like I need to check on you."

"I'm fine, thanks."

"Okay, if you say so."

"I say so. How was your call with Garrison?"

"We had a great conversation. He took his niece to your favorite restaurant....The Italian Villa. She told him... wait, Jamie, Are you crying?"

The silence seemed suspicious.....the sniffling was proof.

"Jamie, what's wrong?"

"Sullivan came over and....and....I....I...didn't mean to.....I just missed him.... and now he's gone." She could not bring herself to share the details but she couldn't hold back the tears.

"I'm on my way. Do you need me to bring you anything?"

"Some crazy glue so that I can mend my broken heart and glue my legs shut."

"I always keep some in my purse. I'm on the way."

Reflections

Giving up the goods: Having sex

Jamie went against what she knew was right for her and gave in to desire. It was a decision she would regret instantly and in the long run. Sometimes we decide based on how we feel and later have to deal with the repercussions. Giving up the goods is one of the most common choices that women make that keeps them single. Jamie has also damaged her self-esteem and opened the door for bitterness. In this type situation it's important to have strong trustworthy friends.

Signs that giving up the goods is keeping you single:

- If you are dating someone and he only wants to have sex.
- If you are using sex to keep a man interested but he hardly is.
- He's giving you excuses as to why he won't commit but he continues to have sex with you.

Solutions:

- Stop having sex until you're married.
- Create dating standards that protect you from sticky situations like Jamie's.
- Go out on double dates or group dates. Could lessen the temptation.

Okay….so….um…not a whole lot to say here. Panties up, dress down, legs crossed. Y'all last name not the same, he can't have none. You are setting yourself up for heartbreak, anger, bitterness, and all of their friends. 1 Corinthians 6:18 ESV - Flee from sexual immorality. Every other sin a person commits is outside the body, but the sexually immoral person sins against his own body. (Solution….ask God to hide you from men until it's time for you to meet your husband.)

What's The Hold Up?

(#9 Unforgiveness)

"Wow…Jamie that is awful. He hasn't called you?"

"No. Not even a text. Danika this is the third time I've answered your question."

"Unbelievable. I'm so sorry friend."

"Not half as sorry as I am. It all happened so fast."

"He may have planned the whole thing. They do stuff like that."

"Well, let's change the subject if you don't mind Danika. Any plans for the weekend?"

"I'll be hanging with my niece and nephew. I haven't seen them in a few weeks. They love Auntie Danika. What about you?"

"This is the weekend I'm supposed to help Penny plan her mom's surprise party."

"Oh yeah. I forgot that you're a party planner. So back to that joker Sullivan…."

"I don't blame him."

"Why not? He's totally to blame."

"I didn't have to have sex with him, or invite him into my house, or even answer when he called."

"So you're saying he's not the bad guy?"

"I'm saying I made the choices and with every choice there is a consequence, good or bad."

"Well, he didn't have to treat you that way. It was really foul."

"I've learned my lesson and want to move on."

"Move on? Do you…..are you….so he gets to go on with his life?"

"Sometimes it's for the best. Forgive, move on, and live."

"You plan on forgiving him too?!?!"

"I have to. I've asked God to forgive me of my sins and He has."

"You are a better woman than me. I wouldn't forgive that joker because I can hold a grudge. I would probably get Carmen to help him fall down."

They laugh. Luckily Jamie's restaurant hasn't opened for the lunch crowd because they were very loud.

"Danika, are you saying you are still holding grudges against people?"

"No, only specific people like my ex Barry."

"Well, that explains a lot."

"What do you mean?"

"When you don't forgive people, you are holding onto negativity. The negativity will attract negative people and situations."

"I still don't understand Jamie."

"You say you won't forgive your ex Barry right?"

"Yeah."

"I could be wrong but you may be having these bad dating experiences because you're holding onto unforgiveness toward him."

"Interesting theory. I agree, you're probably wrong."

"Well, forgiveness is a choice and God forgives us every time that we ask Him."

"You know how to make a person feel low."

"Not on purpose Danika. I don't want you to keep having these horrible dating experiences."

"So are you saying all I have to do is forgive Barry and things will instantly turn around?"

"I won't say that. I'll just say you need to get rid of the unforgiveness. How does it help you?"

"Whatever. I have to get back to the office. Will you check to see if my food is ready?"

"Sure. I have to get back to work myself. There are a few potential vendors to meet with today."

Jamie heads to the kitchen. Danika closes her eyes and begins to whisper to God because she knew Jamie was right. She didn't bother to turn around when she heard footsteps behind her, it was just Jamie.

"Excuse me Ms. Ellsworth. I'm Mr. McMillan from the Keystone Bread Company. We have a 10:15 appointment."

That voice. Danika recognized it. Silky, sexy, and hypnotic. It could only belong to the notorious Barry McMillian, her ex.

Danika wasn't sure if she should turn around or even if she could turn around. It's been years since she's seen him and there was no guarantee of what would happen. After all, how is one to respond after being deceived, broken hearted, and mistreated? Why was Jamie taking so long? Of all times for Jamie to be a slow poke, this was not one.

"Ms. Ellsworth….."

There was no getting away, nowhere to hide. Why should she? Besides she did nothing wrong. He was to blame. She was the best thing that ever happened to that joker since deodorant. Now would be a good time for revenge. Where was that doggone Carmen when she needed her?

Danika stood up slowly, giving Barry time to enjoy the view. She took a deep breath and turned around.

"I'm Ms. Winter. Ms. Ellsworth will be back shortly."

"Hey. Uh Dani."

"Hi."

"I didn't expect to see you here." There was a long silence as Barry stood mesmerized by Danika's beauty. "How have you been?"

"Great." Danika's stern look was not inviting.

"Wow. You look great." His eyes never looked away from hers; it was like he was hypnotized. "Uh, so, how are things with the real estate company?"

"I closed it."

"Really? Why?"

"I wasn't able to maintain it."

"Oh no. What happened?"

"Are you serious? You're asking me why I no longer have my real estate company."

"Yes. I don't know what happened."

"After the break-up…let's just say I was distracted and couldn't keep my clients. Because of you I lost everything and had to start my life over."

"Oh, am I to blame?"

86

"Yes, you are to blame Barry. It's amazing how you can act as if you're not."

"How am I to blame? You broke up with me."

"This is so classic of you Barry. Everything is my fault."

"Danika, you decided you didn't want to marry me, and called off the wedding."

"I had no choice. You were treating me like trash."

"You mean I wouldn't be your puppet."

"I wanted you to be respectful, Barry."

"You wanted someone hen pecked."

"Where's Jamie with my doggone food so I can get out of here. Never mind, I've lost my appetite." Danika is staring at the kitchen door hoping Jamie was on her way out.

"Dani, I've tried to reach out to you for a long time. I've wanted to iron things out, but you were never willing. I've prayed and asked God to help me find you so we can talk."

"Prayed to God huh? Where was all this praying to God when you were trying to keep me from going to church? I don't believe you know how to pray. We're only here by coincidence."

"It's not a coincidence." They turned when they heard Jamie's voice. She had two plates of food. "I asked Barry to come today because I knew you'd be here. Sorry Barry, I don't need another bread vendor. What I do need is for my friend here to have some closure."

Danika looked at the plate with disgust. "I wanted my food to go."

"I know, but you and Barry need to talk."

"I'll bring back the plate tomorrow." Danika reaches for the plate with even more look of discontent on her face.

"Sit down Danika. You haven't returned the other plates you took." She puts the plates on the table that already had silverware. "Barry I brought you a plate and hope you enjoy it. We won't open for a while so you guys can take your time. I'll be back with the drinks."

Danika looks at Jamie and rolls her eyes. "Take these sharp knives with you."

Barry pulls out a chair for Danika. She walks to the other one, pulls it out and sits down. "If I wasn't so hungry I'd leave."

He smiles and sits down. "Is the food that good?"

She puts the napkin in her lap, bows her head and says grace. Although she wanted to punch Barry's lights out, she was going to make sure she told God how grateful she was for her food. Not that long ago it was hard to afford it.

"I'm glad to see that God is still a strong part of your life Dani."

"Let's not talk about God, okay. You used to give me such are hard time for how I believed in serving Him."

"I know and I apologize for everything. It wasn't my intent to make your life miserable. I was a jerk."

"Go on. I'll stop you when you say something wrong."

"I'm sorry. The truth is when we met; I didn't have my act together. You were a big time real estate powerhouse and I was working part-time in retail while my real estate career was just starting. When you agreed to go out with me, I was on top of the world. You were successful, intelligent, resourceful, a go-getter, and gorgeous."

"Go on. You're still telling the truth."

"Well, when things started to get serious, I wasn't sure if you wanted to stay with me. I had little to offer. I let my ego and the guys get the best of me."

"I never cared about your money, status, education or anything like that. I just needed for you to love God and treat me right."

"That's one thing that I loved about you. You didn't try to change me. I thought YOU would change because I'd seen it happen with so many of my other friends. That's why I pulled back from our relationship. "

"All you had to do was tell me and we would have worked it out."

"When a man's ego is in play, he'll do and say things that make little sense to a woman. So, I didn't say anything. I hoped that I'd figure out a way to handle my shortcomings."

"I see."

"That day when you confronted me about my behavior, I knew it was only a matter of time before you would leave." Barry reaches for her knife and puts it on the opposite side of him. "That's why I asked you to marry me." He slid his chair away from her a little.

"Where is Jamie with those drinks? JAMIE WHERE ARE THOSE DRINKS!" Danika yells in the direction of the kitchen. She needed for Ms. Slow Poke to come on out because Barry may need protection.

"Why are you yelling my name? This is a place of business you know."

"Gimme my drink." Danika took a big gulp of her strawberry lemonade. "Gimme another and make it a double."

"Barry you haven't touched your food. Is something wrong with it?"

"No, I'm doing a lot of talking that's all." He tastes the sweet potato soufflé with caramel sautéed pecans. "Outstanding. This reminds me of how Dani used to make it."

89

"It's her recipe. She helped out a lot when I was starting the restaurant. Let me know if you guys need anything. Danika, what happened to your knife?" She sees it's over by Barry. "Never mind." She giggles and goes into the kitchen.

"Look Dani. I prayed and asked God to give me the chance to talk with you and here we are. Coincidence or not, I'll take it. I know I shouldn't have asked you to marry me knowing I didn't have it together. I also know that it didn't matter to you that I was starting out. I didn't want to lose you so I asked you to marry me. I figured that we could have a long engagement and I'd get myself together in the processes."

"Wow......selfish. What was even more selfish was your trying to keep me from going to church."

"I know. That's why I want to say I'm sorry. I'm glad to see you've moved on and are doing better in spite of what happened. I was sad after the break up, so I can relate."

"How do you know I'm doing better? Please don't say it's because I look good. How about keeping up appearances so people won't know that you've battled with depression and almost committed suicide? What do you know about not being able to get out of bed and function daily then losing your business, home, and savings? Tell me about having to move in with your friend and work in her kitchen because your panic attacks wouldn't let you work anywhere else? I'd guess you know nothing."

"You're right. I know nothing about those things. All I know is I would like for you to forgive me. The past can't be changed but, I do know that by not forgiving people can open the door to all kinds of negativity. I don't want you to have to experience any more negativity because I was a jerk. If you choose not to forgive me, I understand. All I can do is ask."

Dani paused, and stared at her plate, and said something silently to God. She looks up and sees that Barry is starring in her eyes. "I have already forgiven you. It's the right thing to do. God forgives me when I've asked so who am I to not forgive you?"

He puts his hand on her hand. "JAMIE….WHERE'S DESSERT?" Danika yelled at the top of her lungs and slowly pulled her hand away. Barry laughs. "I get it. Too soon huh?"

"A little."

"May be we can get something to eat sometime. You know to just talk."

"We already are."

They laugh.

Reflection

Unforgiveness: Choosing to not forgive someone.

Danika was unforgiving toward her ex-fiancé. The years of unforgiveness made it difficult for her to let go of the past. If she forgave, then she probably would have had have better thoughts about relationships. In turn she probably would have met a better caliber of men because what we concentrate on, we get.

Signs that you have unforgiveness:

- You choose not to forgive (sometimes it's that simple).
- Every time you see or think of that person, you have negative things to say.
- If you can't stop talking about why you dislike someone (reliving the past).

Solutions:

- Choose to forgive (some things need to remain in the past).
- Find the lesson(s) in the situation.
- Speak with someone who is in a position to help you figure things out.

How can we expect God to forgive us when we won't forgive. Matthew 6:14-15 ESV- For if you forgive others their trespasses, your Heavenly father will also forgive you but if you do not forgive others their trespasses, neither will your Father forgive your trespasses.

Girl You Look Busted

(#10 Not Looking Presentable)

It was a sunny Saturday afternoon and Penny had nothing scheduled except house work and a visit from Danika. This was unusual for her since she always kept a full social calendar.

John Coltrane began playing which meant that her phone was ringing. It was a matter of finding it. She normally kept up with it but when she cleaned the house, sometimes she could make a mess before she finished cleaning.

As she moved closer to the coffee table the music seemed to get louder. The phone was under the magazines.

"Hey Lady." Penny answered just before it stopped ringing.

"Penny Fab….what's happening?"

"I'm doing house work, girlfriend."

"You're doing housework?"

"Yes, the Fabulous can do things for themselves you know."

"Of course you can. It's just hard to believe you do the things we regular people do."

"Regular people huh?"

"Yeah. Anyway I'm just confirming our time for this afternoon's party planning meeting."

"We sure are. I really appreciate your help."

"No problem. I can't stay as long as I thought I would, so we're gonna have to work fast."

"Is everything okay?"

"Yea, I have a few plans later." Danika was smiling while she said this.

"Why are you smiling?"

"Ok, you dragged it out of me. I might have dinner with Barry."

"Oh my word! Not THE Barry. Barry the ex? Mr. I can't stand your guts?"

"Yep the one and only."

"How did this happen?"

"Jamie scheduled a surprise meeting at the restaurant yesterday and we talked for a bit."

"Is this possibly a rekindling situation?"

"No…not at all. Besides, didn't you tell us we should never accept a last minute date?"

"Yes, I did. So why are you accepting it?"

"I'm accepting it to get closure. I believe I'm sabotaging my own happiness by not clearing up the past. Besides, it's not an actual date with romance and flowers and stuff."

"Well, well, well. Look at God! Danika, I'm so proud of you."

"Thanks."

"This calls for a celebration. I'll make my world famous 'Fabulous Friend' cake."

"Awesome Penny thanks. So did you have time to look at those color swatches for the party?"

"Yeah, I went with the…Oh no, I left all the party material at work!"

"That's ok. We can just use what I have with me and finish the rest next week when you go back to work."

"No ma'am. This has to get done today. Mom's retirement party is a priority and I want to get as much taken care of as soon I can."

"Okay."

"I'll get the stuff. I'm almost finished cleaning anyway."

"Penny, sweetie you don't have that kind of time."

"What do you mean?"

"You're slow when it's time to get dressed to go somewhere."

"Whatever. I'm not slow. Well, maybe at times."

They laughed because there was no way for Penny to deny that Danika was right.

"Okay Danika. There may be a bit of truth to your accusation. I can't help it if I'm meticulous about my style of dress. After all, I am a fashion blogger."

"You don't say."

"How about this? I'll finish cleaning, then run to the office and get the stuff."

"Do you mean go out in public in your Saturday Sweats?"

"Yeah. I'll be back in no time. Besides, there aren't a lot of people in the building aside from security and a few folks here and there with other companies."

"Penny. Wait a minute. You can't go out in Saturday Sweats especially after cleaning. This is dating cardinal rule number.....well, I don't remember which number it is but I'm sure it's in the top 5. *Always Look Runway Ready When You Leave the House.*"

"I'm aware of that but I've already procrastinated about this party long enough. It has to get done today."

"How about I help you clean when I get there and you just fix yourself up."

"I could be on my way back with the stuff by now instead of yacking with you."

"Okay, if you say so. I'll see you in a bit."

Penny turns on some music to make the cleaning not seem so boring. She turns to a station that plays songs from the 90's. One of her favorite songs has just started. She'll be done in no time.

....

After two and a half hours, Penny is finished with the house work. She notices that there is enough time to get to the office and back before Danika arrives. Heading to the door, she passes a mirror and realizes she does need to get dressed but at this point it's too late. Danika was right about dating cardinal rule number 5 and Penny's being slow to get dressed.

Penny arrived at the office building in no time. Saturday morning traffic was scarce compared to the week day commute. No wonder some people came in on Saturdays to get stuff done. She checked her face in the rear view mirror, put on lip gloss and headed to the entrance. The revolving doors showed her reflections and she did not like what she saw. She looked frumpy and unkempt, especially with the scarf and a pony tail poking out in the back.

As she entered the building, she saw Alton Graham the security guard.

"Good morning Mr. Graham. Welcome back."

"Good morning Ms. ...."

"Penny...Penny Fontaine from the sixth floor....from *B. Fabulous Magazine.*"

"Oh right. Ms. Penny. I didn't recognize you."

"I was in the middle of cleaning and had to come back and pick up something."

"Well, all right. It's good to see you too."

"Did you enjoy your vacation?"

"It was wonderful. Me and the Mrs. went to visit our son and his family. Thank you for asking."

"I'd love to hear about it one day next week okay?"

"All right, that will be just fine."

Mr. Graham was an older retired gentleman who worked as a security guard for the building. She had grown quite fond of him because he shared his life's wisdom. Sometimes at work when she wasn't pressed for time, she would bring lunch to share and they'd chat for a while.

She got in the elevator and was at the sixth floor in no time. Luckily she was one of those who had keys and didn't have to get permission to enter the office after hours. Besides being seen by a coworker right now would be embarrassing. She reached her office, grabbed the party material and was back at the elevator in less than five minutes. "That's what I'm talking about." She danced a little as the elevator doors closed.

It slowed down and stopped on the fifth floor. The Capital Agency was located there.

The doors opened, and she became frozen in her tracks. Stepping on the elevator was the finest man she had seen in a long time. He was tall, very handsome, athletic build, and wearing a nicely trimmed beard which she really liked.

"Good morning." Penny batted her eyes and stood in the "*you're about to get your world rocked sir*" stance. She reached to run her hand through her hair. When her hand touched the scarf she almost fainted. She had forgotten that she was in her Saturday Sweats. "Have mercy God." She prayed. "Let him not have his contacts in or something. I look so busted."

"Good morning." He had a deep voice and piercing eyes.

There's no way she could say anything else to him…..no way. Hopefully he wouldn't say anything else either. She stared straight ahead and rode in silence. They would be in the lobby in no time.

"Your article last month was really good Ms. Fontaine." Penny noticed he had a nice smile too. Slow behind elevator….now she had to talk to him.

"Really? Thanks a lot. How did you know who I am? We've never met."

"No. We've never met but you have a column in one of the most popular women's magazines and you're a blogger. It's my job to know who the most successful, intelligent, and beautiful women in this city are, especially when we work in the same building."

Yes….Mr. 5th floor was on point. "Thanks." What else could she say? She couldn't even look him in the eyes.

Ding. They arrived at the lobby and the doors were slow to open. She could hardly wait to get off.

"I have to admit that I don't normally read your column or blog. My sister does, and she creates her wardrobe based on your suggestions. So when it's her birthday, I check out your suggestions and go shopping based on that."

She walks out hurriedly. "How resourceful."

"I don't know if you offer personal fashion consultations but whatever your fee is, I'd gladly pay if you would work with my sister for her new job."

"I don't think so. It was nice meeting you."

"It was nice meeting you too Ms. Fontaine. By the way, I think you look just as lovely in person. Enjoy your weekend." Mr. 5th floor headed toward the doors at the side of the lobby.

Penny headed toward the doors at the main entrance passing the security guard station again.

"Mr. Graham. I'll see you next week. Enjoy your weekend."

"All right Ms. Penny, will do. Before you leave can I tell you something?"

"Sure. What is it?"

"I don't mean to over step my bounds but I feel like I should say something."

"Winston is a nice young man. You've caught his attention."

"Who is Winston?"

"The young man on the elevator with you."

"Oh really?"

"Yes. I could tell by the way that he looked at you and the conversation. I've been around here for years and he hardly ever has any personal conversations with anyone other than me."

"Why is that?"

"He's focused on achieving his goals. He doesn't socialize with people in the building. Small talk yes, elevator chit chat sure, not sharing information about his family to someone in passing."

"So why did he share with me?"

"He's interested in you. He likes what he knows and sees."

"Mr. Graham. I'm in my Saturday Sweats. How can he be interested in me like this?"

"Like I said I've been around here for years. He's been watching you for a while. Not like a stalker but more like a man who evaluates and studies something worth investing in. Also, he's asked questions from time to time. I've never shared anything that you and I've discussed though."

"If he was all that interested, then why didn't he ask me out."

"The expression on your face was saying I can't wait to get off this elevator. "What man would want to ask a woman out when she doesn't seem interested."

"I am interested. I'm just not presentable. It's hard to be fabulous when you're looking busted."

"Apparently he didn't mind. Maybe the next time you come out, you'll be dressed like you could meet someone. You never know who you might run into."

"That's good advice Mr. Graham. Thank you for sharing it."

"Anytime Ms. Penny, anytime."

Penny heads for the door. She saw her reflection and promises to never be this woman again. She steps outside and stops dead in her tracks. It's Garrison. He's walking with some woman who looked like she'd been reading *B.Fabulous Magazine*. What makes it even worse is he had his arm around her. Suddenly there's a knot in the pit of her stomach. She didn't know if it was from seeing him with another woman or from him seeing her so busted.

Is this really happening again, in the same day? There was no way to avoid him. She looks at her phone in hopes he would not notice her. It should work since she was not her fabulous self.

"Hi Penny." Fabulous or not, Garrison was able to spot her.

"Hi Garrision." She didn't even look up. How could she? She looked busted.

"How have you been?"

"Fine. How about you?" She looked up. Those eyes, those eyes.

"I've been doing great. Are you working today?"

"No, I had to get something that I left yesterday."

"Okay."

"So, what are you doing on this side of town?"

"We've been looking at houses and grabbed some lunch."

"That's nice."

"Oh how rude of me. Penny this is..."

"Garrison I've got to be going. I have company coming over and I need to get back." Her mind kind of went blank. She almost didn't care about sounding rude. She couldn't handle him introducing her to his girlfriend. House hunting...hmph! She was supposed to be going house hunting with him, not this modeling school reject.

"Sure. No problem. Maybe...."

She left without hearing what was next. Why did her car seem so far away? Were they still watching or had they gone on? Those really weren't the questions she wanted answers to. Who was the model-looking woman? Had Penny kept him waiting too long, and he moved on? Did Winston think she wasn't interested? How long was she going to let the past affect her future?

She thought about those questions on the ride home. As she pulled into the drive way, Danika pulled in behind her.

"Miss Penny. You have perfect timing. I had my speech ready if you had kept me waiting."

Danika followed Penny into the house. "What's wrong?"

"I could kick myself for going out like this. I didn't realize how the way you dress affects your self-esteem."

"What are you talking about?"

"I met a guy in the elevator. Top shelf fine, okay. I couldn't even carry on a Penny Fabulous conversation. I may have missed a chance to get asked out."

"Wow."

"When I got outside, I ran into Garrison."

"Whaaaat?"

"He was with some floozie."

"Really? Wait. Wasn't he at your office two months ago or something?"

"Yeah. He told me he was ready to settle down, and I needed to let him know something. I guess, my silence told him all that he needed to know."

"Wait one minute. Why haven't you responded?"

"Fears about being married. I've never known one happy couple. The things I've witnessed growing up left me with a bitter taste in my mouth about committed relationships."

"I'm the last person to give advice about marriage. However, God has all answers so tell Him about your concerns."

"You're right friend. I'll do that. Let's get started on this party because you have a date."

"It's not a date."

"What is it?

"I don't know but....well...stop asking so many questions. I gotta finish up and get ready for my date."

They laugh.

Reflection

Not looking presentable: Not dressing as if you care about how you look.

Penny "Fabulous" Fontaine was the cover girl for a fabulous woman. She was always impeccably dressed in the latest fashions coupled with her on sense of style. Receiving stares and compliments were a daily occurrence and didn't move her in any way. She believed her appearance reflected how she felt about herself and others would take her seriously. It was common practice for her to educate her friends on the importance of always going out in public looking your best. The one day she didn't practice what she preached was one she regretted. She met a nice gentleman and ran into the love of her life with another woman. At a time like that she needed to look her best but instead looked less than. This experience was an eye opener not just about always looking presentable but to not assume he will always wait on you.

Signs that not looking presentable may be keeping you single:

- If you have a habit of throwing on anything and not caring how you look.
- You don't smile… Regardless of how you're dressed it makes you look unapproachable.
- If you wear styles that are not flattering….they don't represent your "fabulous".

Solutions:

- Make sure you are always presentable when you leave home.
- Find a style that works for you. You may need to consult a stylist.
- Wear clothes and accessories that make you feel fabulous.

If we are Queens expecting royal treatment from our King, then we must dress like it. Ester1:11 ESV – To bring Queen Vashti before the King with her royal crown, in order to show the people and the princes her beauty, for she was lovely to look at.

Pump Your Brakes

(#11 Saying "I DO" Before He Even Asks)

Jamie was laughing so hard she could hardly shoot the ball into the hoop. This was exactly what Gavin had hoped would happen. His plan was working.

"Stop making me laugh Gavin." She got the words out between chuckles.

"I have to do something. You're beating me at basketball. I cannot let this happen."

"Face it. I'm better than you."

"No way. I'm the best at all the games in this place….even the kiddie games."

"Whatever chump. I'm the best." She sank another ball into the hoop.

"I will win so many tickets; they'll change the name of this place to *King Gavin Coles' Castle of Games and Fun.*" He did an animated dance to stress his point.

Jamie erupts into laughter. It wasn't because he did a retro dance but because it wasn't a very good dance. He didn't seem to care, which made it even funnier.

"I know I don't dance well, but as long as you're having a good time then I'm okay."

Gavin was always thinking about her before he thought of himself. That's one thing that she liked about him. It was one reason she went out with him. This was their fifth date, and she's just as impressed now as she was on the first date.

"Are you ready to eat, giggle box?" He gathered their tickets and put them in his pocket.

"I sure am. I gotta run to the bathroom first."

"Okay….I need to wash my hands too. Meet me at the hostess station when you're done pretty lady."

Inside the bathroom she giggled, as she remembered Gavin's dance moves. She couldn't help but smile when he came to mind. For the first time in a long time, she is on a date with a gentleman. That's what makes him different that anyone she's dated in a long time. She looked in the mirror while washing her hands. Her hair was perfect.

As she's leaving the bathroom Carmen calls. "Well hi there friend."

"Hi J, what's going on?"

"I'm out with Gavin."

"Oh yeah? You two have been seeing a lot of each other. I'm so happy. I really am."

"I'm happy too. He's so nice, thoughtful, and generous."

"I can tell by your voice you're happy. It's good to see you happy for a change Jamie. Wait, if you're out with him, why are you on the phone with me?"

"He's in the bathroom."

"Where are you?"

"We're at the arcade."

"The arcade….that's cute."

"It was his idea. He's always taking me to special places to show how much he's into me."

"How does he do that?"

"Are you serious? We're at the Family Fun Center. Why else would he bring me to a place like this if he wasn't trying to let me know he wants kids? Also, he's probably trying to see how I'd behave around them."

"Are you serious, Jamie?"

"Listen to the places he's taken and tell me he isn't trying to tell me something. Date #1 *The Red Bistro*. It's between two flower shops and across the street from the tuxedo shop."

"Wooow, love is in the air." Jamie didn't notice the sarcasm in Carmen's comment.

"I know right...Date #2... I told him my favorite color was blue, and he took me to a jazz concert at the *Blue Trumpet*. Everyone knows that's where all of the fabulous wedding receptions are held."

"Yeah they are, but..."

"Date #3....He took me to a cake-decorating class. He decorated his cake like a blue ring box. Cake.... Ring box...Something Blue.....Hello!"

"Now, Jamie, don't you think you're reading too much into it?"

"Why else would he take me to those places and do those things? He's so sweet, caring, and thoughtful."

"Maybe that's just how he is. Why not enjoy being out with a nice guy and if it becomes something more, then great."

"Carmen. You don't know what it's like to get rejected time and time again. It doesn't matter if I play hard to get or even have sex, I get rejected. This time it's different. It's like he's giving me subtle signs. I've been praying to God to send me someone special and here comes Gavin."

"God heard you and Gavin could be that someone. But you're saying "*I Do*" before he even asks. Let me give you some advice."

"You don't have to."

"Here it is anyway. Follow his lead. If he's not showing interest in being serious then don't assume he is serious. Enjoy his company. If later you find out he's not someone you'd get serious with then make sure you tell him asap."

Jamie is silent.

"Jamie."

"I'm here. I'm trying to swallow all of that. It's really a lot to hear while on a date."

"I didn't mean to say anything upsetting."

"It's okay. I gotta go anyway. I'll talk with you later."

"All right. Enjoy your date."

Jamie felt a little frustrated. Carmen was the last person to give anyone dating advice. She couldn't keep a man, so how was she in a position to tell anyone else about how to keep one.

Gavin was at the hostess station with one hand behind his back and a big smile on his face. He always made her feel better with just a smile. That's one thing she liked. There was genuineness about him. His smile was authentic.

"I'm hoping I didn't keep you waiting long. My buddy Carmen called."

"Is everything okay?" She looked frustrated.

"Yeah it is. She uh...uh... she never said what she wanted."

"Okay."

The hostess approaches them. "Right this way."

"After you Madame."

"Thank you sir."

"I told her we'd like a booth. A table would have taken 30 minutes."

"That's fine."

"Here you are. You're server will be with you in a minute. Enjoy."

They slid into the booth and Gavin made sure whatever he had behind his back remained out of sight. He grabbed a cloth napkin from the table and covered it.

"What are you hiding over there?" Jamie's eyes are as big as her smile.

"Oh, a little something for you. I'll show it to you later."

"It's for me? You are so thoughtful Gavin. Thank you."

He winked and it was like a garage door opener had been pointed at her lips. She gave him the biggest tooth paste commercial smile.

Jamie looked down at the menu and the discussion with Carmen flashed through her mind. She couldn't help what she was feeling or thinking. "He's giving me a gift. If he wasn't thinking about being serious, then why was he doing 'just because' type things?"

The waitress interrupted her thoughts. "Hi, I'm Sierra. I'll be your server today. What can I get you to drink?"

"I'll take lemonade."

"Okay sir. How about you ma'am?"

"I'll take water with lemon."

"Okay. Would you like to start with an appetizer?"

110

"Yes. We'll have the mozzarella cheese sticks and mild Buffalo wings. Did you want something else Miss Jamie?"

"No."

"I'll put your order in and be right back with your drinks."

"I hope you don't mind my ordering the appetizers."

"No. It's fine. Women like it when men take charge."

"Really?"

"Yep."

"I see."

"We feel special. Every girl wants to feel special. You know what I mean?"

"Hmmmm. Well, I don't know what that's like but I'll accept your opinion. Just like I hope you'll accept this." He picks up the thing that he had behind his back. It was a small teddy bear with a top hat and tuxedo coat. He hands it to her.

"Oh Gavin. This is adorable. Thank you so much. She admires it and gives another garage door opener smile."

"I redeemed the tickets while you were in the bathroom. It was really the only thing suitable for a special young lady like you."

"Really? You know. Gifts say a lot about the giver."

"How is that?"

"It tells what they were thinking about."

"Interesting. What does the bear say about me?"

"Says you are very glad you met me and can't wait to have your own top hat and coat."

"I'm not sure I understand. Explain a little more."

"You are ready to get serious with me. Giving a stuffed animal is usually how men show interest. A tuxedo and top hat are usually found at weddings. Those two say you're ready to be serious."

"Jamie, I really like you. There are so many things about you that make it easy to hang with you. However, I can't say I'm ready to get serious with you. If I were, I would tell you."

"Okay. I didn't mean to make you uncomfortable." She looks down at the menu.

"I apologize if I've hurt your feelings."

She didn't reply nor look up. Here it goes again. She made a fool of herself. When will it end? She was embarrassed and could feel that knot in her stomach.

"Jamie..."

"Oh sure. I accept. I'm kinda used to it."

"Used to what?"

"Used to being interested in someone who is not interested in me."

"Jamie. I didn't say I wasn't interested. I'm not ready to be serious and wanted to be upfront."

"I understand."

"I don't think you do. I believe in courting a lady. Yes, it's old fashioned but there is an art to dating and it's hardly practiced now-a-days. I was taught that when you court a lady, you're learning about one another. As you learn one another you can tell if you're a good fit or not.

112

From there you can determine if you should continue to date. Taking things slowly can prevent messy situations."

"I've never heard it that way. It makes sense."

"Let's take it day by day and see what happens."

"I'd like that. Thank you for being honest with me."

"You're welcome."

Sierra walks up with their orders. "Here are your drinks and appetizers. Are you ready to order?"

"Sure, I'll take the Chicken Alfredo." He hands Sierra his menu.

Jamie folds her menu and hands it to Sierra. "I'll take the chopped chicken salad with ranch dressing."

"Okay….I'll put your orders in." Sierra puts the menus on the tray and leaves.

"Do you mind if I say grace? I learned to thank God for my meals."

"No sir, not at all."

Gavin reached out for her hands and blesses the food. "Father, thank you for this food we are about to receive. Thank you for the hands that prepared it and the nourishment it provides for the body. Thank you for the wonderful company I'm enjoying today. In Jesus name…Amen."

"Amen. Thank you for blessing the food Gavin. Saying grace is something you don't see in public."

"In public or in private, it gets done. I'm too grateful to God not to thank Him."

"I know that's right." She puts a few of the appetizers onto a plate and puts it in front of him. This time he has the garage door opener smile.

She winks. That was a move Penny taught her. Showing you are selfless can help build a solid friendship with a man.

Their phones buzz at the same time. They check them and chuckle.

"Carmen texted if he doesn't wash his hands or say grace leave immediately."

"My cousin Kurt texted, if she doesn't wash her hands or say thank you for saying grace, make her pay for her own food because she is not the one."

They laugh.

"Those were interesting texts." Jamie puts wings on her plate.

"Yes ma'am they were. Kurt will be happy to know I'm picking up the check." He winks and passes her a few napkins.

Reflections

Saying "I Do" Before He Asks: Assuming he is your future boo-boo based on signs, hints, or your gut feelings. Also, it means acting as if he is going to be your husband without him asking you to marry him.

Jamie wanted a relationship more than just about anything. It was obvious in her actions. Gavin may be exactly what she needs. He's someone who recognizes that they needed to take things slowly. Many times people can be so ready for love that they jump the gun and over look or refuse to see warning signs about the other person. Then later there is a lot of regret, heartache and tears only to finally see what had been there the whole time.

Signs that you say I do before he even asks:

- Shortly after meeting, you are thinking about marriage (or talking to your girlfriends about it).
- You hint around to him, about marriage before he's even mentioned where you stand.
- You express negative feelings towards him when he doesn't share the same feelings about marriage as soon as think he should.

Solutions:

- Wait for him to talk about marriage. (Be careful if he's mentioning it really soon after meeting.)
- Stop telling your girlfriends everything about your dates. (Co-signing isn't always good.)
- Pace how you date. Establish what time frame you'd be comfortable getting serious, if you're into him like that.

Dating has so many uncertainties; it's good to have patience. Most of the time, we want what we want when we want and how we want. The issue is our potential mate may not know what they want or how to express it. This can easily cause us to be impatient. Anything done as a result of impatience usually is coupled with regret. Romans 8:25 ESV – But if we hope for what we do not see, we wait for it with patience.

Friend, Bookey, or Mr. & Mrs.

(#12 Not Knowing Your Date Category)

Penny ran into Winston in the elevator again one day after work. This time she was 100% Penny "Fabulous" Fontaine, impeccably dressed. She wore a *B. Rose* designer dress, handbag, and shoes, which weren't even available to the public yet. To top it off, she also wore *B. Exquisite Parfum* by *B. Rose,* which was $300 a bottle. It was all a gift from the designer *B. Rose* herself. Being an award winning Fashion Blogger had its' benefits; besides her job was to look photo shoot ready.

She decided that never again would a day go by where she would not be appropriately dressed in public. Penny learned a valuable lesson that Saturday. It wasn't just *always look runway ready* as she so often spouted to her friends. It was *practice what you preach.* Fortunately the meeting with Winston in the Saturday sweats was not a deterrent. When they met again on the elevator, it later turned into *let's meet for coffee.* Later coffee turned into *would you have lunch with me?* Lunch evolved into *I'd be honored if you'd accompany me to……*

Penny and Winston enjoyed each other's company. A few months after meeting, Winston asked to date exclusively. They were on their way to becoming a power couple. Invitations to the cities' most prestigious events poured in regularly. The latest invitation was for a charity auction at the Carousel Foundation.

"Did I tell you that you look beautiful tonight Ms. Fontaine?"

"Yes, Sir Winston you did." She smiled as he opened the door for her. When they walked into the Carousel Building it seemed as if everyone was staring at them. A photographer from the newspaper took their picture. Penny posed and smiled as if everyone had showed up to celebrate them.

"Thank you for inviting me, Winston."

"You are welcome. I wouldn't have come with anyone else."

Winston always made those type comments. When he did, it made Penny feel "Fabulous".

"Everyone looks so nice. Although there are a lot of fashion no-no's here." Winston shook his head. "I'm sorry. It's a force of habit. I am a fashion blogger."

"How about let's leave work at work and enjoy the evening."

"I can handle that."

"Let's walk around and bid on some of these items." He offered his arm.

They walked a few minutes and came up to a small statue that caught Winston's eye. He began to exam with the eye of an art aficionado. The artist was local, which made the piece even more appealing.

"This is a magnificent piece. The artist has captured the essence of the model." Winston looked like a kid in a candy store. All of this was way above Penny's level of understanding and interest. However, she enjoyed watching Winston in his element.

"A magnificent piece indeed! I will be sure to tell the artist that his work is being enjoyed by one of the cities' premier art collector." It was Catherine Von Austantine.

"Catherine. It's nice to see you."

"It is nice to see you as well Winston. Gerald was just asking about you. Where did my husband run off too? Honey, over here." She waved to get her husband's attention.

Gerald made his way through the crowd and extended a handshake to Winston. "Winston. How are you? I was just asking Catherine about you. We're so glad that you could make it."

"I'm glad to be here and to be able to help your organization Gerald."

118

Catherine turned to Penny and extended her hand. "Hi, I'm Catherine."

Winston realized he had not introduced Penny. "I apologize. Catherine, Gerald this is Penny Fontaine."

"Hello, it is a pleasure to meet you both." Penny gave her most glamorous smile.

"Winston, we are so glad you and your beautiful girlfriend could make it."

"We're just friends, and yes she is beautiful."

Penny was shocked to hear him say that. Her faced was evident. Catherine saw Penny's expression and thought she and Winston may need to be alone.

"Gerald, there's the Mayor. Let's say hi. Winston be sure and checkout the piece next to the stairs. Penny it was nice to meet you."

"Nice meeting you too, Catherine." Penny had forced a smile on her face. As the Von Austantines left, so did the smile on Penny's face.

"Penny, are you ok? You look flustered."

"Yes, I'm fine. Well …. I'm not sure."

"What's wrong?"

"We've agreed to only date each other right?"

"Right."

"You told Catherine that I wasn't your girlfriend but just your friend. I'm confused. Are we or are we not in a relationship?"

"Do you want to talk about this here?"

"Yes."

"Sure, whatever you want."

"I'm confused about what's going on between us. I thought I was your girlfriend."

"I've overheard you mention to one of your friends you may want to get married. I don't want to get married. So, I don't see the need for us to be in a committed relationship."

"Why haven't you said anything about it, Winston?"

"You never said anything to me. I figured I wasn't a candidate."

"I followed your lead. Were you planning on us only dating?

"Yes. Penny, I was married before and realize it is not for me. As long as you want to go out, we can. I will continue to date only you."

"I understand."

"I'll leave it up to you. You don't have to decision right now. Let me know if you change your mind."

"Sure. Will you excuse me? I'm going to the lady's room."

"It's right over there. I have to place a bid on the piece I was looking at. When you're done, how about meeting me at the staircase?"

"Okay, I will." Penny tried to make her voice strong and neutral. She barely passed it off.

She went into the lady's room, sat on the couch, and breathed deeply. Wow, what a shock. She would have continued to think they were a couple, if Catherine hadn't called her his girlfriend.

Carmen was calling. "Hi Carmen."

"Eeew. Why do you sound like that?"

"I have a reason."

"What's wrong? Aren't you out with Winston tonight?"

"Yes, we're at an auction for the Carousel Foundation."

"You enjoy auctions, so what's wrong?"

"I found out he doesn't want to get married."

"So, why do you feel bad? You don't want to get married either. At least you know where things will go."

"Yeah but, when I saw Garrison with that modeling school reject…"

"Stop calling her that."

"With that woman, I had second thoughts. It wasn't necessarily about them, but about me not wanting to be alone forever. Garrison had shown me what I needed to see to take a chance on love. I let my fears get in the way. He's with someone else now and I can deal with it. However, I can't deal with wasting my time or someone else's. That's what I've done by dating Winston. I can't keep seeing him knowing that he doesn't want to get married."

"I see."

"Go ahead and give me your insight. Whenever you say I see, it means you've got some type of revelation."

"Penny, you can't say you've wasted time dating him because you've enjoyed every minute."

"True."

"You now know where his mindset is regarding marriage. So you can continue to date him but control your feelings. That's why it's important to know why you are dating when you date someone. As time goes along if you find out they don't want to get married or at least get serious, then you may need to make adjustments."

"You are absolutely right. I must confess I'm pleasantly surprised to hear that from you."

"Penny, I'm aware of the dating rules. I didn't know them back in the day, which is why I endured so much heartache. It later became bitterness. I don't want you to be anything other than your fabulous self."

"Thanks, Carmen. I'm going to go and find a nice piece for your mantle. Your advice was worth it."

"Okay bye."

Penny freshened up her makeup and left the lady's room. She decided to get a drink, and smiled because there was no line at the bar. "Good evening ma'am what can I get for you?"

"She'll have a glass of orange and pineapple juice, light on the ice."

No need to turn around. She knew who it was…Garrison. He stood so close that she could smell the new men's fragrance *B. Real* by *B. Rose*.

"How are you Penny?"

She turned around. There he was, in all his fineness. "I'm great Garrison, how are you?"

"I'm okay."

"Why just okay?"

"I don't know, just okay."

"I understand."

"You look beautiful… but that's to be expected."

"Thank you."

"I saw you having a conversation with a guy but didn't want to interrupt."

"He's a friend." Normally she wouldn't have explained, but it was Garrison. And after all, as of five minutes ago, Winston was *just a friend*.

"It's so good to see you Penny."

"There you are Garry, I.....well hi, Penny!" It was the lady who was with Garrison when she saw him outside of her office building that Saturday.

"Hi." Penny didn't know what else to say. She wanted to ask fifty questions and leave at the same time. To see Garrison with someone else was tearing her up. At that moment she knew she wanted to be with him. It wasn't because of Miss Lady. He made his way through the crowds of people, despite who he was with. He's always been the kind of person to maintain a friendship unless you say otherwise.

"It's me Penny. Marlene. Marlene Turner. I mean Tinkie."

"Tinkie??? Oh my gosh. I didn't recognize you."

"Most people don't. I've lost a lot of weight, lost the glasses, cut my hair, and created a *B. Fabulous* wardrobe."

"You look great. It's so good to see you Marlene."

"I wanted to speak with you when we saw you that Saturday. You seemed to be in a hurry."

"I was.... well, I apologize for my behavior."

"We were looking for Garrison's new house. Not only am I his favorite cousin, I'm also his realtor."

"That's awesome."

"I think I found one I like. Maybe you can see it one day next week." Garrison hoped that she would say yes.

"I'd like that."

"Good evening everyone." Winston walked up next to Penny and spoke to Garrison and Tinkie.

"Hi, I'm Marlene." She handed him a business card.

"Garrison." He shook hands with Winston.

"Winston Bannister." He could tell there was a connection between Penny and Garrison. He looked at Penny. "Are you ready?"

"Sure. It was good seeing you guys." Marlene hands Penny a business card. "Call me so we can have lunch."

"Yes ma'am. I look forward to it."

Winston extended his arm to Penny. They headed to check out other auction items. There was no need for her to look back because she knew Garrison was watching. Winston knew it too, so he released her arm and put his hand on the small of her back, giving her big smile.

Penny had a lot to think about.

Not knowing your dating category: Not having a clear reason why you are dating. Are you dating for fun, companionship, or marriage? These are the dating categories.

Penny was not sure if she wanted to be married or not. She'd witness things growing up that did not give her assurance that marriage is a good thing. However, after finding out where she stood with Winston, she needed to make a decision about her future. It's important to know why you're dating so you won't waste time with someone who has a different dating agenda.

Signs that not knowing your dating category is keeping you single:

- You have not determined why you're dating (you can always move to another category)
- You continue to date someone when all signs show you don't share the same dating agenda.

Solutions:

- Determine why you want to date.
- Be aware that sometimes men will shift to another category and have a new dating agenda. Be prepared for that. Pay attention to the signs because there usually are some.
- Realize that as long you don't have a dating category, you may continue to have unsuccessful dating experiences.

This is the area of dating where you should think versus feel. There can be so many uncertainties because we are dealing with imperfect people just like us. Use wisdom especially when dating someone who has a different reason for dating. James 1:5 ESV – If any of you lacks wisdom, let him ask God, who gives generously to all without reproach, and it will be given him.

God Has The Answer

The ladies gathered at *The Foxfire* for lunch. Their schedules had been so hectic they hadn't been able to meet like normal. There was a lot of catching up to do.

"Good afternoon, ladies." Aaron is the waiter who serves them for lunch. He is professional and has a pleasant personality.

"Hi there Aaron. How are you?" He always gave them a five star dining experience.

"I'm well Ms. Fontaine. Would you ladies like your usual drinks?"

"I'd like to try the white grape fizz today." Carmen saw blank stares. She never tried new drinks. "Why is everyone looking at me?" She had the biggest smile and her eyes sparkled.

"Hmmmm…What's going on Carmen?" Danika noticed Carmen's sparkle immediately.

"You're trying new drinks, you're wearing a new perfume and your makeup is different."

"Instead of worrying about what I've got going on, how about telling Aaron what you're drinking." Carmen may have made a few changes but her quick wit was the same.

Danika giggled and sat back in her chair. "Aaron, I'll have the usual."

"Me too." Penny pushed away her menu. She was more interested in what was going on with Carmen.

"All right ladies, I'll get your drinks."

"I'll take my usual too, Aaron thanks. Hey you guys. Did I miss anything?" Jamie always arrived last.

"Nope." Carmen turned the page in her menu hoping Danika wouldn't repeat what she's noticed. She knew her hoping was in vain.

"Yes, there is." Danika was smiling and looking at Carmen.

"What's going on Carmen?" Jamie hadn't noticed anything yet.

"Nothing is going on. Danika here is making a big deal of my new perfume, that's all."

"No ma'am. You have a new hairstyle, new makeup, new shoes and you're smiling." I noticed as soon as I saw you. It's my job as a fashion blogger to pick up on these things. Penny reached out, touched Carmen's blouse, and examined the stitching. "Is that *B. Rose?*"

"Just because I've put on a new blouse and perfume doesn't mean something is going on. Can't I show what I've learned by reading your fashion blog? It is *B.Rose*....so what."

Aaron was approaching the table but instead of drinks he had a bouquet of beautifully wrapped flowers.

Penny waived to Aaron. "Over here. They must be from…."

"Sorry, they're not for you Ms. Fontaine." Penny's smile was replaced by disappointment.

The others were shocked because Penny always received flowers.

"They are for Ms. Roster." He hands them to her with a large smile.

Everyone gasped, even Carmen. She never received flowers. As she looked them over and read the card, her smile grew even bigger.

"What's going on? You said I didn't miss anything, but I believe I did." Jamie leaned in trying to sneak a peek at the card.

"Okay. They are from Carlyle Monroe." Carmen folded the card and tucked it back into the bouquet.

"Carlyle Monroe the sportscaster?" Penny hoped it was.

"Yes, he is. Penny, please don't tell me that you used to date him."

"Oh no, I've never dated him. We met a while back and I see him at various functions. He's a nice guy."

"Why are you getting flowers from Carlyle?" Jamie could hardly wait to hear the story. This was good news. "You are going to tell us right?"

"Of course she is." Danika knew Carmen would tell. This was something she wanted to share and now was as good of a time as any.

"I met Carlyle a while back in the grocery store. He asked me on a lunch date."

"Carmen, I can't believe you've been going out with Carlyle this whole time and you never told us." Danika shook her head.

"We haven't gone out much. When we met I freaked out and dissed him."

"Okay. So, I'm lost here. Tell us what got you to the point of receiving flowers in a restaurant." Penny was confused but intrigued.

"After I turned him down in the grocery store, an older lady approached me. She saw the whole thing and told me that my past pains would keep me from happiness. I saw her again a few more times and she always said the same thing."

"That was God. He has a way of getting your attention. I know all about it." Danika was always the first to acknowledge how God looked out for her.

"Okay ladies. Here are your drinks. Are you ready to order?" Aaron passed out the drinks and pulled out his order pad and pen.

"I'll have my usual please." Penny handed Aaron the menu. Danika and Jamie gave Aaron their menus and asked for their usual. "I think we'll all have our usual."

"How do you know I want the usual?" Carmen tried to cover her smile with the menu. "Sometimes change is good."

"Okay Ms. Roster what will you have?" Aaron moved closer.

"I'll take the usual." They all laugh.

"I'll put your orders in." Aaron took the menu and went to the kitchen.

"Carmen, tell us more about Carlyle, the older lady and how you got these flowers." Penny was all smiles. She couldn't wait.

"I was volunteering at the Food Closet and was partnered with the older lady. The entire three hours was like a therapy session. At first I didn't have a whole lot to say because I felt some kind of way about her."

"Why did you feel some kind of way about her? You didn't even know the lady."

"Jamie, you know how I can be. Every time I had a run-in with a guy, she was right there and had something to say. I didn't want to hear it. She was telling me the truth about me and my possible future."

"So what happened at the Food Closet?" Danika grabbed her napkin. She felt herself becoming emotional.

"After about a half hour of silence, I asked the lady did she remember who I was? She said she did. Then I asked her why she gave advice all of those times. She asked God to allow her to help women avoid the pain and loneliness she faced. Her story was common. She was in love with a man who broke her heart. Instead of asking God for help, she let the hurt become anger and bitterness. Every man afterwards paid for what the first man did. She ended up with no husband or children. The turning point was when she asked God to take away the pain. He told her she had to forgive the guy. It took a while but she chose to forgive and now has peace and a nice gentleman friend."

"What did you take away from all of that?" Penny nibbled on a hot roll.

"I knew exactly what she said that day in the grocery story after I met Carlyle was true. My past was hurting my future. My anger and bitterness toward one man was going to cause me to be alone for the rest of my life. I didn't want to be alone so I knew I had to ask God what to do. I found scriptures about anger and forgiveness. Every day I spoke positive confessions about my life and made a lot of changes. As you can see, I changed my wardrobe, I eat healthier, and I laugh more. I just did a total overhaul. I didn't want any part of the old way anymore. Once I felt better and thought I had myself together, I told God what I wanted in a mate."

"He did say He'd give us the desires of our heart."

"You're right Danika. That's why I told Him. I also told Him I wanted who He thought was best for me. I've made a lot of dating errors in the past and didn't want to make any more. A few weeks later I ran into Carlyle at the grocery store again. I apologized and went on about my business. We ran into each other again at a function and spent a few minutes talking. After that we seemed to bump into each other around the city. Eventually he asked me out. We've been going out for a while now and it's been fun."

"So what's next for you guys?" Danika dabbed the corner of her eye, she had gotten a little misty.

"We're just taking it one day at a time for now."

"I absolutely love it!" Penny was the first to show her enthusiasm. She leaned over and hugged her friend.

"Forgiveness is a powerful thing. It is so freeing." Danika reached for a roll.

"Um Ms. Lady is there something that we need to know?" Jamie eyeballed Danika with a smirk on her face.

"Nope."

"Liar. You're eyes are dancing. I recognize that look." Carmen felt qualified to make the announcement since she had dancing eyes too. "Do you have a new boo-boo?"

"No, not new. I've been going to lunch with Barry."

"Are you serious? You can't be serious. We haven't seen anything on the news about it." Penny loved being facetious.

"I came here for lunch one day. Jamie had him to come and speak with her about being a vendor. We talked a bit and now we have lunch sometimes."

"That's amazing....that's God. It's not a secret that you despised him and now you're having lunch. I'm proud of you." Carmen knew how hard it was to get past the pain of a broken heart.

"God is awesome isn't He? When I chose to forgive Barry, I saw how I was only hurting me. I truly believe that my unforgiveness was attracting bad dates. Well, regardless of what happens with us, I'm glad to no longer have unforgiveness. I'm also thankful for Jamie risking her life by setting up the meeting." They giggled.

"You are welcome. I'll do anything for my girls."

"Oh yea? Why don't you tell us about your friend Jamie?" Penny raised her eyebrows and sipped her drink. "You didn't think we wouldn't find out, did you?"

"Who told you about Gavin?"

"You just did." Penny snickered. She had a way of finding out what she needed to.

"His name is Gavin Coles. It's amazing how easily we hooked up. I say amazing, because you guys know how I usually do when I see a guy I like."

"Nope, tell us about it." Danika was being facetious.

"Danika stop playing. You know I used to chase after men. I didn't give them a chance to ask me for my number or dinner or anything. I always tried to help them see I was a good catch."

"What changed that? Did you have an older lady to tell you about yourself like me?"

"Carmen, I asked God to tell me what I was doing wrong. He brought back to my remembrance the wisdom of my grandmother. All my life, she would give me wisdom about men. One thing she said was, when a woman pursues a man, she is not letting him be a man. According to her, men are hunters by nature and get a since of fulfillment when they get their lady. Of course it has to be done in their time and way. If we don't allow them to hunt us then there's nothing for them to look forward to.

"Wow that is deep. Your grandma has a lot of wisdom."

"Yeah Carmen, you're right. I'm blessed to have her share with me."

"So, how did you meet and stuff?" Penny was buttering another roll.

"He came into the restaurant and I conducted business with him. That was it. He came back quite a few times for work and to eat. After a while he told me that he enjoyed talking to me and asked if we could talk over coffee. I agreed and we've been seeing each other ever since. The good part about it is that I'm okay with us just hanging out. If we become more than friends then fine. If not, then that's fine too."

"My girls are growing up so fast." Penny pretended as if she was wiping away tears.

"You are so silly. So uh-rum what's the 411 on you?" Jamie pointed her finger at Penny to let her know the spotlight was on her.

"I don't....I don't think I should get into that. The food is here and we need nourishment." She let out a snicker.

Aaron directed the waiters to their destinations. "Ladies, here are your usual meals." He poured more water into their water glasses. "Let me know if you need anything else." The waiters followed him to the kitchen.

"Now back to you Penny. What's going on with you?" Jamie unfolded her napkin and put it in her lap.

"Ladies, I don't have a lot of new things to share. However, I will tell you this. For love and relationships, I've seen a lot of negative things. That's why I've never been committed to anyone. When I saw Garrison with another woman, I knew it was too late for us. I also knew that I didn't want to be alone for the rest of my life. Telling God my concerns was all that I could do. I realized that I had to listen to and trust Him, whether I had someone or not. He would always show me what I needed to know about whom ever I was dating."

"So are you dating someone or not?" Carmen couldn't stand the suspense. Jamie, Danika and Penny smiled. Penny sipped her drink.

"Good afternoon ladies." Garrison strolled past Carmen and stood next to Penny with a bouquet of flowers.

"Good afternoon Garrison." They spoke in unison with big smiles.

He handed Penny the bouquet and kissed her hand. "I don't mean to interrupt. I just wanted to drop off a little thinking- of-you gift. I'll see you later." He was gone just as fast as he came.

"Um yeah. I guess my question is answered and then some." Carmen opened her napkin and put it in her lap with a really big smile.

133

"He's good to me. All that I had to do was trust God. It seems to me ladies that the answer to our situation was with God the whole time. We just need to trust Him for the answers in His time."

They nodded in agreement.

"I'd like to say grace." Carmen reached her hands out and everyone joined hands. "Father, we thank you for another day. Thank you for your love, mercy, and grace. We bless your name and give you praise. We thank you for friendship, this food, and for your son Jesus dying for our sins. Where we would be without you, we shudder to think. We give you glory and honor in Jesus' name. Amen."

"Amen." They repeated in unison.

"Ladies, I have been asked to find women for a photo shoot for the *B. Fabulous Magazine*. The photo shoot is featuring career women. They asked me if I could recommend any women and I recommended you guys. If you don't want to do it, it's fine."

Carmen gave thumbs up since her mouth was full of food.

"Sure." Danika posed and smiled as if she was taking pictures at that moment.

Jamie raised her glass. "Ladies, I propose a toast." They raised their glasses. "Here's to friendship, new beginnings, power moves, the love of God, and no longer being single against your will."

Author's Notes

I hope you have been enlightened and entertained. Someone asked me why I chose *"twelve"* things that keep women single against their will. I just stopped at twelve, no particular reason and certainly there are more than twelve. For example *Not Being Seen*. If a woman always goes to the same places like work, mom's house, home; work, church, home; work, grocery store, home, she's making it hard to meet men. (Another example, *Getting All of Your Advice From One Source*.)

If you do not identify with any of the twelve reasons listed, it's okay. Take a moment to reflect on your past relationships, dating habits, and beliefs on dating. The answers you seek may be there. This is important because ladies, it's not always the man's fault. Also keep in mind that there is no such thing as a perfect man when it comes to dating. You can have a perfect dinner or night out on the town but he will not be perfect.

I'd also like to say, although this book is fiction, I can identify with a few of the situations. The one thing that helped me through my negative dating experiences was my relationship with God. It wasn't enough to believe in Him but to be His child. I say I have a relationship with God because I've asked Jesus to come into my life and be my Savior. If I didn't have a relationship with God I don't know how I would have made it through those dark times.

I encourage you to accept Jesus as your Savior today. It's not just about being able to go to Heaven when you die but having the Almighty guide you on earth. You can't be concerned about what others may say or what you've seen or heard about "Christians/Church folk". People will do what they do, so you can't make life decisions based on them. Try God for yourself.

If you want to try Him for yourself, just say this prayer aloud and mean it from your heart. Jesus I believe that you are the Son of God and you died for my sins. I believe that God raised you from the dead and I confess you as my Lord and Savior. I am saved. (Romans 10:9)

Remember that if you reflect upon your attitudes, beliefs, and behaviors about dating, you don't have to be single against your will.

Scriptures quoted are from wwww.openbible.info.